Dear Mystery Reader:

Irene Allen and her cu[illegible] n
Elliot are back with Q[illegible] e
outside, Elizabeth is a [illegible].
A retired widow wh[illegible] l
Quaker meeting, she a[illegible] e
for the Cambridge, Massachusetts Quaker community. She's also full of energy and has an infectious personality. Through her we not only get an insider's look at Quaker life, but an insider's look at a very un-Quaker act. Murder.

The second DEAD LETTER addition to this critically lauded series finds Elizabeth traveling to Seattle to visit a friend. Elizabeth is all set to spend quality time with her old friend Reba Nichols when, much to her surprise, Reba vanishes. Elizabeth teams up with a young doctor named Meghan to investigate, and, to everyone's horror, it turns out Reba has been brutally murdered. And if that weren't awful enough, Elizabeth finds her own life in danger, forcing her to hunt down a killer before she becomes the next victim.

If you enjoy QUAKER INDICTMENT, you'll be glad to know that due to her overwhelming DEAD LETTER success, we're bringing previously out of print Irene Allen mysteries back into print. In the meantime, check out her first DEAD LETTER mystery, QUAKER TESTIMONY. You'll be glad you did.

Yours in crime,

Joe Veltre
Associate Editor
St. Martin's Press DEAD LETTER Paperback Mysteries

Other titles from St. Martin's **Dead Letter** Mysteries

FAMILY SKELETONS by Rett MacPherson

AGATHA RAISIN AND THE TERRIBLE TOURIST by M. C. Beaton

MOTHER NATURE by Sarah Andrews

A LONG WALK UP THE WATER SLIDE by Don Winslow

THE HOUSE OF THE VESTALS by Steven Saylor

MOODY GETS THE BLUES by Steve Oliver

THE TOYOTOMI BLADES by Dale Furutani

THE GARDEN PLOT by J. S. Borthwick

BLACK DIAMOND by Susan Holtzer

LET IT BLEED by Ian Rankin

THE CASE OF THE HOOK-BILLED KITES by J. S. Borthwick

ON THIS ROCKNE by Ralph McInerney

AN UNHOLY ALLIANCE by Susanna Gregory

NO COLDER PLACE by S. J. Rozan

THE RIDDLE OF ST. LEONARD'S by Candace Robb

A MURDER IN MACEDON by Anna Apostolou

STRANGLED PROSE by Joan Hess

SLEEPING WITH THE CRAWFISH by D. J. Donaldson

THE CLEVELAND LOCAL by Les Roberts

WHILE DROWNING IN THE DESERT by Don Winslow

Dead Letter is also proud to present these mystery classics by Ngaio Marsh

ENTER A MURDERER

NIGHT AT THE VULCAN

SPINSTERS IN JEOPARDY

A WREATH FOR RIVERA

Panda grabbed the sleeve of her jacket in his teeth, clenched hard, and pulled her forward. Just before Elizabeth regained her wits enough to shout at the dog, one of her feet was obstructed by something on the ground.

The stumbling block, as it were, was soft and warm.

Panda released Elizabeth, and the old woman simply sat down in the dirt. She gingerly reached out and felt the slick nylon fabric of Meghan's ski jacket. The young woman's nearest shoulder was covered with a sticky liquid.

Meghan groaned softly.

"Meghan, wake up!" said Elizabeth, putting into her voice all the stern, warning tones she had used as a mother. "Stay awake, do you hear me?"

"Yeah, I hear," answered Meghan. Her breath was now both audible and deep.

"Where are you hurt?"

"Just a graze to my shoulder. I'm OK."

"No," said Elizabeth firmly. "You're not OK. You are lying in the darkness on the cold dirt, drifting in and out of consciousness."

Somewhere in the great, dark distance Elizabeth thought she heard the sounds of a helicopter in flight.

Also from St. Martin's Paperbacks

Quaker Testimony

Quaker Indictment

QUAKER INDICTMENT

IRENE ALLEN

St. Martin's Paperbacks

QUAKER INDICTMENT

 For information address St. Martin's Press, 175 Fifth Avenue, New York, N.Y. 10010.

Library of Congress Catalog Card Number: 97-31615

ISBN: 0-312-96684-9

Printed in the United States of America

St. Martin's Press hardcover edition / February 1998
St. Martin's Paperbacks edition / January 1999

10 9 8 7 6 5 4 3 2 1

For Ruby,
a neighbor and fellow Downwinder

Acknowledgments and Author's Note

Many friends and relatives have helped me with this story. My mother was especially useful, accompanying me during a visit to the Hanford site. Her kindness toward me on that trip is more than I can fathom, but I am glad to accept her help. Looking back at my sojourn to central Washington, the friendly residents of Richland and the grandeur of the free-flowing Columbia River stand out in my mind as clearly as the images of nuclear reactors and surreal warning signs.

This is a work of fiction, and the people and events within it are the products of my imagination. In the spirit of storytelling, I've taken the liberty of moving the Benton County sheriff's office back to the county courthouse in Prosser, where it used to be. I've also set up the main security office for Hanford in the 300 Area. Finally, I've entirely omitted both Kennewick and Pasco, not owing to any disrespect for these fine cities but to help simplify what a reader unfamiliar with the geography of Washington State must master. Other than these points, however, I have tried to leave Hanford and its environs as they truly are.

Hanford's history, as mentioned in these pages, is quite factual. The record of radioactive emissions, both intentional and unintentional, and the current problems administering the site can be studied in more detail through articles in *The New York Times*; the Seattle, Portland, and Spokane newspapers; and any of several books published in recent years.

The reader might be entitled to know that I think the radiation emitted by Hanford has likely been less harmful to almost everyone in the region than has the site's long history of deceiving the public. The lies the government and its contractors blithely broadcast for decades have been searingly corrosive. In that sense, residents of central Washington and Oregon are still paying a heavy price for the Cold War our nation waged for so many years around the globe.

Prologue

Darkness reached up to her, and Elizabeth feared she would pitch forward into the abyss. Her head was spinning, her heart constricted in agony. But her eyes remained open, automatically darting around the bloody scene at her feet. Never had she felt so far from home, so distant from the life she knew in New England. And never had she felt so far from what she thought she had known of the Spirit's love. Elizabeth's mind, now furiously racing, flashed into deep anger against her lifelong religious faith.

"Can you identify this body?" asked the sheriff at her elbow. His voice was low but insistent.

"Yes," answered the Quaker as she turned away from the corpse. She staggered and would have fallen to the gravel had the enormous lawman not instantly steadied her.

"How did I ever come to this?" murmured Elizabeth to herself just before rage once again washed through her mind.

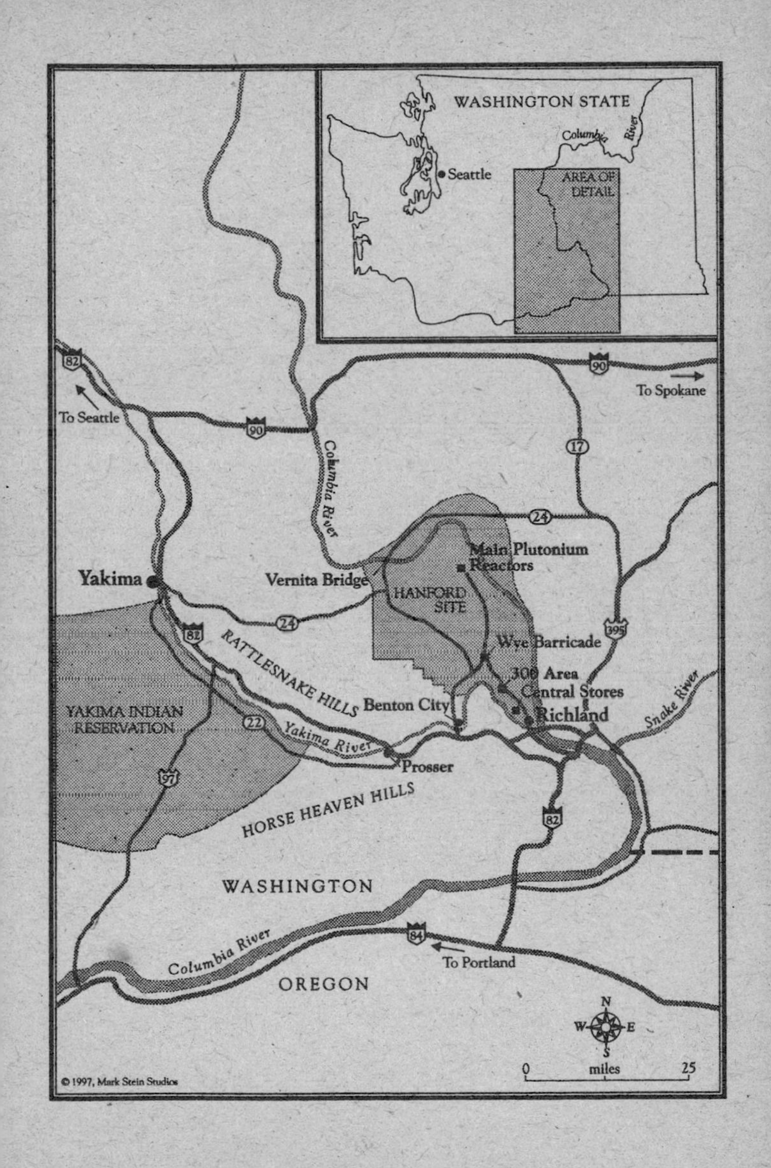
WASHINGTON STATE
Columbia River
Seattle
AREA OF DETAIL
82
To Seattle
90
To Spokane
Columbia River
17
24
Main Plutonium Reactors
Yakima
Vernita Bridge
HANFORD SITE
24
82
395
RATTLESNAKE HILLS
Wye Barricade
300 Area
Central Stores
Benton City
Richland
YAKIMA INDIAN RESERVATION
22
Yakima River
Snake River
Prosser
97
HORSE HEAVEN HILLS
82
WASHINGTON
Columbia River
84
To Portland
OREGON
N
W
E
S
0
miles
25
© 1997, Mark Stein Studios

1

Sometimes we must leave our fixed abode and become sojourners in uncertainty. We need to learn that no place, however hallowed our memories, is more holy than any other. The earth is the Lord's—the whole earth. Wherever we go, God is with us.

Elizabeth Watson
Twentieth-Century American Friend

"You are free to move about the cabin," said the flight attendant's high and scratchy voice over the plane's intercom. "The captain has turned off the seat belt sign."

Elizabeth Elliot left her seat belt firmly in place, low and tight across her lap. A few minutes previously, the plane had flown through what the captain's deep voice had informed the passengers was "mild turbulence." To an inexperienced flyer like Elizabeth, the rocking and jerking of the airplane had been impressive, and she had no desire to leave her seat whatever might now be permitted.

Elizabeth was on her way from Boston to Seattle to visit Rebecca Nichols, her closest friend from college days. Their mutual collegiate life was forty years in the past, but their friendship remained as strong as ever, and Elizabeth had been looking forward to this trip for months. She had never seen the Pacific Northwest. She wanted to drink in all she could of the place, so distant from New England, and spend lots of time talking with Reba as well.

Elizabeth smoothed her navy-blue linen skirt and stretched back in her window seat, trying to ease the sharp but familiar arthritic ache in her lower back. Looking out the window, she was relieved to see that the Great Plains were coming to an end. The ground was now decidedly uneven, with swelling, broad hills cut deeply by creeks. To a Yankee like Elizabeth, the terrain below the airplane deserved to be called mountainous, but she knew that in the West the standards for alpine status were higher than they were in New England.

The huge expanse of rolling grassland below her was sobering and a bit disorienting to someone who had lived her whole life in the Boston area. She wondered what sort of person inhabited the land over which she was so lightly skimming.

What would it be like to shape the contours of your life in such a barren, treeless land? thought Elizabeth. *More importantly, how long could I remain a Quaker without the support of Friends' community around me?*

"Beer, wine, or a cocktail!" barked a flight attendant in the aisle, leaning over the empty seat next to Elizabeth and raising her voice.

Elizabeth was startled by the interruption of her contemplative thoughts, but she answered quietly and steadily. "No, thank you kindly." As a lifelong teetotaler, she always replied with those words when more worldly people asked—or tried to dictate—what sort of alcohol she wanted.

Reading her passenger quickly, the attendant responded, "We have soda, ma'am, if you'd rather."

"I would very much like a cup of tea," said Elizabeth. She was unsure whether something so simple could be obtained on a gleamingly modern airplane. Earlier in the flight, she had declined a plastic basket of cellophane-wrapped food, and she was concerned that another point of anomalous behavior would cause trouble for the hardworking young woman standing beside her. Still, what she wanted was tea, and her desire was strong enough that it led her to an uncharacteristically direct request.

"It'll be brought up from the back," answered the attendant briskly.

She pushed a button over Elizabeth's head and made a *T* sign by crossing one hand over the other, looking as she did so toward another young woman in the aisle at the back of the plane. In about a minute, a cup of lukewarm tea appeared at Elizabeth's elbow. She sincerely thanked the attendant and sipped what tasted like Lipton's instant.

In her well-ordered home in Cambridge, Elizabeth Elliot would have poured lukewarm instant tea down the sink. But suspended high over the immense and barren earth, with the jet engines' roar only a few seats behind her, she was truly grateful for what she had received. The flight from Boston, the confusion of changing planes in Chicago, and the experience of turbulence had worn her out. Tea of any description was, in Elizabeth's mind, quite possibly heaven-sent.

Five minutes later, Elizabeth was feeling more relaxed and cheerful. She rummaged in her purse for Rebecca's most recent letter and reread her old roommate's neat but tiny script:

Dear Elizabeth,
If I get this into the mail today, I am sure it will reach you before you leave Cambridge. I want you to understand why I'm so glad you're coming. (It's always a joy to see you, but your coming this month is just perfect.)

Last winter, my 92-year-old mother died in a hospital in the city of Richland, in central Washington State. It was thyroid cancer. Her last two years were very painful because of the disease—and because of the doctors' treatments. Cancer is no surprise in someone so old, of course, but it was also cancer that took my father—as you will remember, I think—back an eon ago when we were at Wellesley. And leukemia killed my younger sister about five years after that. I'm afraid that malignancies of one kind or another are all too common near my home. While she was still in her more sprightly 80's, my mother got involved in a group that was compiling information about local cancer rates. It was quite an education for both of us. But I'm getting ahead of myself.

My mother's death left me sole heir to my family's house and land outside Richland, and that's my main concern now. In recent years there's been quite a bit printed about the federal government's Hanford nuclear site, which is also in central Washington, literally within sight of downtown Richland. Hanford has had a long history of impacting (as they say) the area around it. That means all of Benton County—and our counties out west are huge, not like in New England.

I hope you've seen some of the articles The New York Times has run recently about the Hanford property. Established just north of my hometown of Benton City during World War Two, it was the place—the only place in the nation—where plutonium was made. That required specially designed nuclear reactors, all built in a great hurry in 1943 and 1944. There are still hulking nuclear reactors at Hanford on the banks of the Columbia River, left over from those days. During the Cold War, the amount of plutonium that Hanford produced just grew and grew because it was a key ingredient in all American nuclear warheads.

Throughout that time, more reactors were built—and quite a bit of radioactive debris was released into the air at Hanford. It drifted across the area and moved downwind. The government, no matter how you look at it, systematically covered up information about those leaks. At one point the boys in charge of the place even made the radioactive emissions quite deliberately, to see if farm animals in the area died. They didn't warn the local residents.

As a Quaker, you probably think that's the normal mentality of the military, but really it's not supposed to work like that. Innocent civilians (our own citizens, no less) are not supposed to be used as nuclear guinea pigs, especially without their consent. Remember, the U.S. was not even at war! I realize all this may be hard for you to fully believe (unless you've been keeping up on this from afar, which maybe you or your Meeting has been doing). But I'm not exaggerating, Elizabeth: the Hanford authorities shortened at least some civilian lives in Washington State, and they always did so with public assurances that nothing radioactive was escaping the Hanford grounds themselves.

To get back to my own story: after my mother's funeral, I stayed in my family's house (where she had been living until shortly before her death). Our land is too dry to be farmed, and it's never been irrigated, so there's not much beyond sagebrush and tumbleweed on it. The property is just outside the tiny town of Benton City. My cousin owns some land there, too, although not so much. As it happens, my parents' land literally borders the southern boundary of Hanford. I realize I should sell the place, but it seems evil to sell what may be a toxic and dangerous property. The next owner could be affected like my family was, since some of the radioactive things (I guess "compounds" is the right word—the terminology is complex for a banker like myself) are still on the land.

So: I gathered three soil samples from my property and took them home to Seattle. After a week or two I found a chemist at the University of Washington who would test the soils for various types of radioactivity. The chemist, Professor Wenzel Bloch, found what he calls "interesting" values but he wants more than three samples before he'll give his scientific opinion about the hazards that may be on my property. (I had thought three samples was a lot when I gathered them, but he says it's a small number. They all came pretty much from the same place. You can't generalize, he says, from that. "Statistical insignificance" or some such.)

I've got time off at the bank whenever I want it, and when you get here we can drive over to the center of the state and follow up what I've begun. I'd like you to be there for moral support, not for any sample digging—I'm in good shape still, and I know your arthritis is bad. You'll be a real help to me because your strict conscience can guide my pragmatism. I shouldn't sell the place if the soil is harmful to human health, should I? But what is to be done with the property when I'm gone? Our government is surely no help!

Don't worry, there will be things other than nukes to see here in Washington. You'll like the Northwest—everyone does. And it's so good of you to come all this way!

I'll meet you at the Sea-Tac airport when your flight comes in.

All my love until then,
Your roomie,
Reba

The topic of the letter was a challenging one, but that was no surprise to Elizabeth. Rebecca was a responsible person, and she was not one to meekly accept a bad situation. When they had been roommates, so long ago, both women had been serious students. That was the key characteristic they had in common, and that was how they had grown to respect each other, despite marked differences in temperament. Elizabeth had always had a withdrawn, other-worldly approach to life, while the commanding Miss Nichols was quite the opposite. Rebecca formed opinions and took action as easily as she breathed. She was a natural leader. Elizabeth knew that Rebecca Nichols could be a serious thorn in the side of the government authorities if she so chose.

Setting the letter in her lap, Elizabeth took off her reading glasses and again looked out the airplane's window. Snow-covered mountains were now spread in glowing sunlight beneath her. The beauty was arresting, and she lost herself in the view. Some of the ridges below her were razor sharp, and a little snow had accumulated on them. In those places, she could see dark rock, sometimes with still darker bands within it.

The sun was directly ahead of the plane, to the west, so the mountain peaks cast shadows eastward. Elizabeth realized with a start that it must be already dark in Cambridge. She was surprised she could be so far away from home so quickly. Scolding herself about her disquiet, she shook her head firmly.

There's no reason for me to be anxious, she thought. *I made the connection in Chicago, I'm on the last airplane I have to face today, and dear old Reba will meet me at the airport as soon as we land.*

Nevertheless she felt quite alone. She almost envied Sparkle, who had been left at home in a cat-loving neighbor's care. Watching the Rockies slide beneath the plane, Elizabeth disciplined her thoughts as best she could by considering the nineteenth-century journey of Lewis and Clark over these mountains. She had read Lewis's journal in school half a century previously, and her memory of things she had learned early in life was much sharper than her memory of all too many recent events. She knew that the Lewis and Clark party had come through the country beneath her in the late summer, somehow getting themselves and their gear over the challenge of the high mountains with horses purchased from the Indians. Even airplane turbulence and fears of being so far from home could be seen in perspective when she recalled the sufferings of the explorers.

The intercom snapped to life with a sprinkle of static. "This is the captain. We're just passing south of Glacier National Park. We're making up the time lost by our delay in Chicago, and the weather in Seattle is looking good."

The majestic scene out her window convinced Elizabeth at a glance that the national park program was one of the best things the federal government had ever done. This thought was followed by the recollection of Rebecca's letter and what it communicated about other government activities.

Elizabeth Elliot, numbed by the noisy cabin, the tiring events of the day, and her senseless anxieties about travel, lost herself, first in thought, and then in a confused, light sleep.

Forty minutes later, another mountain range was passing beneath the plane. Elizabeth awakened and looked at the stunning set of peaks.

This must be the Cascades, she thought.

She tried to ease her arthritis pains and her wrinkled clothes by moving forward in her seat and straightening her shoulders. But she couldn't take her eyes off the window next to her.

Unlike the Rockies, the Cascades were wearing a partial mantle of clouds. But the larger peaks were fully visible above the white fluff, standing proudly well into the sky, almost as if divorced from the Earth beneath them. The plane began to descend as Elizabeth tried to determine which of the several peaks might be Mount Saint Helens. Although New England Yankees might not know a great deal about the Northwest, Saint Helens was famous even in the East for its eruptive temperament. The red glow of the sunset was becoming intense and the scene was exploding into a dark orange beauty when Elizabeth's window was covered by a gray-white curtain of clouds.

The captain put on the FASTEN SEAT BELT sign.

2

The Society of Friends . . . became the first sect to embody a concept of the equality of men and women within its church government and discipline, liberating Quaker women to preach and prophesy . . . (this) prepared them for leadership roles when the time was ripe for a women's rights movement to emerge . . .

Margaret Hope Bacon
Twentieth-Century American Friend

Rebecca had met Elizabeth, taken her to a tastefully decorated downtown apartment, and joyfully fed and fussed over her old friend. They had laughed about their increasingly similar appearance. Both had left behind the hair color of youth and had silver-gray curls instead. And although Rebecca still was the taller of the pair, she had picked up a few pounds in recent years, gaining the sturdy silhouette Elizabeth had acquired decades earlier after giving birth to her children.

Now, in the low light of early morning, the two women were leaving Seattle, Rebecca at the wheel of her dark blue Saab. Following her friend's lead, Elizabeth had dressed in slacks rather than a skirt. She didn't feel able, however, to wear a turtleneck top as her northwestern host advised. Her white blouse, with two pleats in the front, was 100 percent cotton, and although she had ironed it before leaving home, it was wrinkled from its journey in her suitcase. With a heavy cardigan in her hands, the old Quaker had gratefully, if stiffly, sunk into the passenger seat of the immaculate Swedish car.

The leather bucket seat promised to be much more comfortable than what the airline had provided the previous day, and Elizabeth was relieved to feel her stiff back relax slightly.

Under Rebecca's firm direction, the car soon crossed a long, floating bridge across a large and beautiful lake. Then they cleared the sprawling city of Seattle, and the highway climbed gently but steadily toward the Cascades. The mountains were straight ahead, lit from behind by the early morning sun. A ruggedly symmetrical volcanic peak, seen briefly through a great valley, loomed to the southeast.

"That's Mount Rainier," said Rebecca, "Washington's most majestic peak. At least in this native's opinion."

"It's only early October," mused Elizabeth aloud. "Is it unusual to already have so much snow at the top of the mountains?"

Rebecca laughed gently. "You're not in Kansas—or should I say Cambridge—anymore, my friend. Peaks in the Cascades are snowcapped year-round. And, from what I heard on the radio yesterday, we'll find some snow even down here on the highway once we get near the pass."

Small pines grew thickly along the road. Rebecca explained that the diminutive trees were new growth, following a clear-cut by a timber company some twenty years earlier. She related some parts of the complex relationship among the timber industry, which employed many people on the west side of Washington; the federal government, which owned the land the trees grew on; and the growing lobby of environmentalists, which had its power center in Seattle's middle class. Elizabeth didn't understand it all, but she gathered that her friend closely followed the timber debates that dominated state politics. Elizabeth knew many Cambridge Quakers who professed quite extreme conservationist views, gladly calling themselves "Green" and holding forth on logging practices across the country. She wondered, as the car climbed gently up and up, how Quakers might view the timber industry if their livelihoods depended on lumber rather than on the well-paid professional jobs that most Cambridge Quakers took for granted.

She sat up sharply when a thin layer of snow appeared under the pines out her window. The snowy blanket grew more substantial as they rapidly gained elevation. The hills around them had long since turned into what Elizabeth was sure even westerners would call mountains. But the road had been well plowed, and Rebecca seemed to handle the driving easily enough. Elizabeth tried to relax in the hands of her ever-competent friend, a natural executive who was, after all, always on top of the situation. Rebecca Nichols, as Elizabeth well knew, had risen in the male-dominated business world to senior vice president of an international bank with dealings all around the Pacific Rim. Still, Elizabeth couldn't help but have a residual concern about what seemed to her a harsh and wild environment.

Why should simple travel make me anxious? she queried herself in exasperation. *It's quite irrational. And, more importantly, it's unfaithful.*

Above the timberline, the nearest peaks could be seen more clearly. Even though the highway remained safely in the valleys, with the comforting presence of trees to soften the glare of sun on snow, the car continued to climb. Elizabeth felt a sudden increase in her internal adrenaline.

Will I get a migraine from these elevations? she wondered.

Just as she was about to speak to Rebecca about her anxiety, a large highway sign announced that they were at the top of Snoqualmie Pass.

Rebecca, quite unaware of her visitor's distress, calmly observed, "Part one of the drive is behind us. It's downhill all the way from here to Benton County."

The warmth of relief flowed through Elizabeth. As the car descended, the country around the two women became more open, clear of the thick growth of trees that had been on the west side of the pass. The peaks declined, step by step, toward the elevation of the highway. Elizabeth continued to look around her, with something not unlike delight replacing at least much of her apprehension.

"This state's landscape surely changes quickly!" she could not help observing.

"That's the rain-shadow effect of the Cascades. On this side of the range it's dry land, so the timber thins out and disappears. You get the feeling of big, open spaces. And it will be drier yet where we are headed." As the car continued to sweep downhill Rebecca added, "You'll see sagebrush, and then, of course, a lot of dust. That's what I grew up with as a child."

"It sounds like an old western film," said Elizabeth. She added with decidedly understated levity, "Are there cowpokes where we're headed?"

"No," said Rebecca, no laughter in her voice. "These days the only work is with the federal government. That's the whole trouble in a nutshell."

Her jaw was set hard as she lapsed into silence. Elizabeth,

unafraid of a suspended conversation, allowed the silence to continue for several minutes and gazed out the window. Then, spontaneously, she decided to offer her friend a respite from heavy thoughts.

"My son William," she began, "moved away from Cambridge this past summer, Reba. He works now as an engineer in California. I haven't been out to visit him yet, but I imagine it can't be more beautiful than what we've just crossed over."

"Glad you liked it!" responded Rebecca. "As I recall, when we were in college, you thought the Charles River in springtime was the height of natural beauty. I could never agree with you."

"Yes, I remember. I can see now the standards you were judging New England against. It's really apples and oranges, just two quite different parts of the world."

"That's right," replied Rebecca, turning the car's heater off.

"I do still love walking along the Charles in the spring," mused Elizabeth. "And when the boys were young it was a great joy to share those walks with them."

"Everything must be different for you," said Rebecca abruptly. "I mean, having had so many years with a husband and family life. Two sons to your credit—and one's a doctor!" She added the last comment in a teasing tone.

"I'm grateful for them both," responded Elizabeth seriously. "But sometimes I've felt rather inadequate when I look at all that you've accomplished." With clear emotion she added, "I never used my college education as you have, Reba."

The point was something that Elizabeth had often thought

about over the years. She had benefited from college, certainly, but she had not continued the type of intellectual growth that might have been hers if she had pursued a formal career.

"I always felt I should stay home, raise the boys, and work at Friends' Meeting," she continued. "It was all worthwhile, and I'd do it again. But your accomplishments are amazing, Reba, and you did it all on your own, using the talents God gave you and putting the college background we got together to some real use."

Rebecca laughed.

"Banking doesn't take any education, Elizabeth! It's not a profession of eggheads, let me tell you. But, yes, I've risen in the professional world. I've had responsibilities, and headaches, and some small bit of power, and good pay. If that's success, then Wellesley College led me to a successful life."

There was a pause before she concluded: "It's all been worthwhile, and I'm proud of what I accomplished. No, not proud so much as glad I had a chance for all the inner growth that's been demanded of me on my way up. That part of my life has been more wonderful than anything I could have imagined when we were roomies." In a matter-of-fact tone she added, "But no one will miss me when I'm gone, and that hurts."

"Rebecca!" the Quaker exclaimed in a surprisingly sharp voice. "Don't talk that way! Your family and friends will miss you, just as I will be missed by my family and friends. It's true, of course, people will adapt and go on with their own lives when we're gone. That's always the case, and very properly, too, no matter what one does with one's life."

"Well," responded Rebecca after a moment's thought, "you're right. I was avoiding the real issue, I suppose. You see, sometimes late at night, I really am troubled—by something I imagine you'll take seriously as a Friend. I've been successful, yes, and I take satisfaction in that. It's brought me happiness, certainly.

"But you and I know that mere happiness should not be our goal—happiness, or what the young people seem to call 'fulfillment.' This country's cult of individualism—that wasn't what we wanted to join when we were in college, was it, Elizabeth?"

She waved her hand across the view above the dashboard and continued at a higher pitch.

"We inherit so much from those who came before us. Language, for one, especially written language, and all the skills and knowledge involved in agriculture, the basic mathematics that people worked out in the past—" She sneezed.

"God bless you," said Elizabeth, both automatically and sincerely.

"You see what I mean, don't you?" continued Rebecca. "You're an old, old friend, Elizabeth, which is why I feel I can speak this way. We owe it to the world and to God to pay something back for this patrimony we inherited." She concluded more calmly, "That's the way it seems to me. And my happiness in a successful career has not addressed any of that—the notion of giving back."

"I think you're painting with too broad a brush," said Elizabeth quietly. "Remember, our society depends on banks and bankers. We couldn't have major industries without them, which means we couldn't all enjoy the material abundance we do in this country. It's a small thing on a cosmic scale, I suppose, but without a bank loan, Michael and I could never have bought our house. That goes for everyone of normal means. Your work is valuable—just as farming or bus driving are valuable, too."

"Hmmm," responded Rebecca skeptically. "That's nice of you to say, Elizabeth. But the real saints, Mother Teresa and that sort, seem a bit more valuable than the average banker or wheat farmer."

"Not in God's eyes," said Elizabeth firmly. "And I'm sure Mother Teresa would be the first to say so. Besides that, your business position and your worldly skills are helping you, right now, to try to do the morally right thing about these Hanford problems."

"I hope so." Rebecca accelerated and pulled around a truck. Elizabeth closed her eyes, then peered cautiously from lowered lids. When they were beyond the lumbering semi-trailer, she continued with a note of deep certainty in her voice.

"Developing human potential is part of God's plan, Reba, and you, not I, have taken that seriously throughout your life. You blossomed and grew as you were given more and more responsibility at work. Besides that, your career helped advance the status of women in our society. That's much more than a minor point."

"Don't make me a role model for womankind!" answered Rebecca, shaking her head emphatically. "That's too heavy a burden." She paused for only a moment before adding, "But if women like me helped make things a little easier for the next batch of girls leaving college, I'm glad. And you're kind, Elizabeth, to answer me so generously."

"Not kind." Elizabeth shook her head slightly. "That's what I believe. Never, never forget, Reba, that you and others like you have done us all a great service. You helped move our society forward toward equality."

Rebecca pulled off the highway, reluctantly stopping the conversation to say they needed gasoline. "The good thing about driving, I've often thought, is that you can really talk seriously to a person," she said. "But sometimes the conversation gets interrupted right just when it's getting somewhere." She added matter-of-factly, "This is the town of Ellensburg. We're about halfway to my family's land."

Rebecca got out of the car at a gas station. Elizabeth slowly wrestled with her door. Finally it swung partway open, but she wondered how she would get her arthritic spine to unbend.

If a highway emergency crew passes by, she thought ruefully, *I'll ask them to help get me out of this seat with their Jaws of Life*.

In fact, she made it to her feet, even if she moved quite slowly throughout the process. Only after the victory of standing up straight could she tell that her mind was fuzzy from the noise and vibration of the highway. As she slowly looked around, she saw that Rebecca wore a puzzled frown as she read the instructions on the pump, holding the nozzle in her hand.

"It's prepay. It's prepay," said a brisk young man with a tone of authority as he got into a pickup truck at a nearby pump. Elizabeth instantly understood what was at issue and went into the station to give the attendant a twenty-dollar bill.

The man inside was almost Elizabeth's age. He was putting some finely ground tobacco into his lower lip and at the same time humming to the country-music song playing over a battered radio near the cash register. As he took Elizabeth's money, the song reached its chorus:

Yeah, I'm calling 'bout that job in the paper;
No, I don't mind waitin' on hold.
Yes, I'm still here, just praying to my Maker,
Really hopin', you won't say I'm too old.

"Amen to that, eh?" said the cash register attendant, looking at his mature customer.

With a mixture of guilt and gratitude for her own good fortune in retirement, Elizabeth smiled weakly and went back outside. Across the hood of the Saab, Rebecca nodded her understanding of the transaction and started the pump. Standing next to her friend, Elizabeth asked how the economy in the Northwest was faring.

"It's better than it was during the Reagan and Bush recessions," answered Rebecca. "And the Puget Sound area is in fine shape. Microsoft, of course, and all the rest of it. But even the biggest boom in Seattle doesn't help in the rural areas. There is a lot of unemployment, and even more underemployment—even though so many people have given up and left!

"All over the small-town West, life isn't easy. Here in Washington, that's one reason that people put up with Hanford. The place may have been terrible in almost every way, but it's always generated jobs. Good jobs, with real pay, government benefits, and all the rest."

After settling their bill, they departed. The land around them was now dominated by short and spare grass, a few dark rocks, and the occasional steer.

"Is this a desert?" asked Elizabeth.

"No, no," laughed her friend. "This is good land. Soon the grass will pretty much stop, but even then we won't be in true desert!"

After another hour of driving there was, indeed, little grass and no cattle in sight. Rebecca stopped the car on the side of the road.

"Let's get out for a moment for a stretch."

Elizabeth was glad for a chance to straighten her stiff body relatively soon after the last stop. The wind was steady from the west. Both women looked back toward the distant mountains. The sky, Elizabeth realized with a start, looked enormous. It stretched for scores of miles in every direction.

"What big country this is," she said, more to herself than her companion.

Rebecca had stepped off the shoulder of the highway. She came back toward the car, giving her friend a small, silvery green sprig of plant she had picked.

"It's sage," said Rebecca. "Sage and tumbleweeds are the most common plants you'll see from now on."

The Clerk of Cambridge Friends Meeting put the plant to

her nose and sniffed. "Is this the area that you think is more contaminated than the government has admitted?" she quietly asked.

"This is the beginning of it, yes. The soil, the water, everything from here and a couple of hundred miles downwind has apparently been affected."

Elizabeth looked thoughtfully to the east, the direction the wind was blowing. Her heart was heavy as the two women got back into their dark blue car. Perhaps depressing thoughts, or simply the fatigue of travel, helped Elizabeth to nod off as the quiet automobile continued east.

3

It is time we accepted a truth of modern psychology, that people do not act according to what they know, but according to how they feel about what they know.

Rachel Davis DuBois
Twentieth-Century American Friend

You missed the town of Yakima, and the reservation around it," said Rebecca when Elizabeth awakened. "And we just passed Prosser, which is the county seat for Benton County. We're getting quite near my home."

Elizabeth looked with reinvigorated interest at the open country around them. Two huge but orderly ridges flanked the highway at a distance. The dramatically higher ground, like the lower land, was absolutely bare.

"I didn't know that mountains in such a northerly state as Washington could be denuded like this," observed Elizabeth.

Rebecca laughed. "Goodness! They aren't mountains! On our right are the Horse Heaven Hills, and on the left are the Rattlesnake Hills."

"Of course," Elizabeth said steadily, "northwesterners can name their mountains as they wish. But it will take me quite a while to think of those ridges as mere hills."

"We've got plenty of time," responded Rebecca easily.

"What's this?" Elizabeth nodded to a field they were passing. Tall poles, row after row after row of them, dominated the scene. Autumn frost had trimmed back the vines that still clung to the lower portion of the poles.

"The land of milk and honey," answered Rebecca. "Or rather, the land of hops. Most American hops—it's an ingredient of beer, Elizabeth—come from this area. It's all made possible, of course, by the Corps of Engineers' ability to provide water for irrigation. And that's all underwritten by you good taxpayers in the East!"

"Better to pay for irrigation than for the military," said Elizabeth. She scanned the corn and alfalfa fields, soon followed by a field spotted with holsteins. As abruptly as this Eden had appeared, however, it was gone. They sped back into the monotonous, empty desert. Still studying the strange vistas, Elizabeth noted that the Rattlesnake Hills were drawing in closer to them, squeezing the interstate highway up against the hills to the south.

A tiny, battered trailer house on the barren earth slipped by Elizabeth's window. Next to it, two junked cars rested. Just as she was about to internally ask a blessing for the poor family living in such circumstances, an isolated fenced field swept past. Three beautiful horses were running along the fence, parallel to the highway.

"Gorgeous animals!" murmured Elizabeth.

With a glance at the spotted horses, Rebecca nodded. "Appaloosas. Chief Joseph and the Nez Percé relied on them in their flight from the U.S. Army. Good horses in rough terrain. But strong-willed."

"Appaloosas," said Elizabeth aloud, pronouncing the syllables as a mnemonic aid for her increasingly less than perfect memory.

"Named for the Palouse Indians," said Rebecca, "who lived a couple hundred miles east of here on the Plateau. They are extinct—the Palouse, I mean—but the Appaloosa are firmly established in the horse world."

A large black-and-white bird stood on the very edge of the blacktop. It was pecking at roadkill that it held firmly in its feet. The big bird paid no attention as their car roared past only a few feet from it.

"What was that?" asked Elizabeth quickly. She thought she knew her Audubon book, but she had never seen such an entry.

"Just a magpie," answered Rebecca easily. "They'll eat anything, carrion very much included.

"We have a supper invitation at my cousin's," she continued as they turned off the main highway onto a county road. "But we've enough time to stop at my parents' house and clean up."

Just three miles off the interstate they entered a small, dusty community, proudly identifying itself on a large sign as Benton City. It was, to Elizabeth's eye, a poor place: a few solid houses were scattered around, but most of the town was dominated by minimal homes and old trailers. There was no order, no neatness to the place. It didn't take long to pass through Benton City, going north on the one and only road. Then, on top of a low, barren hill to their left, there stood a white clapboard house.

"This is it!" said Rebecca, gaiety and mockery laced into her voice. "The Celestial City we've been seeking!"

The prominent position of the house, combined with Elizabeth's daylong anticipation, gave the Quaker a small rush of energy.

Rebecca pulled up the long gravel drive, and the two women got out of their small car. Rebecca unlocked the farmhouse's front door with some difficulty, explaining that the stiff lock was an original. The air in the house was stale, but that changed quickly as Rebecca propped open the door. They went upstairs, and Elizabeth looked around with interest at the house. Rebecca sorted out a set of towels and linen for them each. She showed Elizabeth which was to be her room. Just then they heard the pure and simple tones of a young woman's voice calling to Rebecca from downstairs.

Going down to the first floor, Rebecca introduced Elizabeth to Meghan Zillann, an attractive younger woman who had long, blond hair braided down her back. Meghan smiled brightly, nodded to Elizabeth, and spoke in a rapid-fire style to Rebecca, all at the same time.

"I'm cheering up a friend, Nancy Davis, who used to be a nurse in our clinic," said Meghan. "We're just coming back to Richland from Prosser. Been finalizing Nancy's divorce—from a real cretin. It's a good day, but still not easy for her. So I thought I'd buzz up through Benton City and see if you'd got in yet. Let me get Nance. She's out in the truck. Can Panda come in?"

Rebecca laughed and nodded as she steered Elizabeth to a chair. Meghan disappeared, but quickly was back with another youngish woman in tow. Before anyone could speak, a long, single-note whistle from Meghan brought a large, black-and-white dog bounding into the room.

Elizabeth, as a cat person, was apprehensive, but the big,

shaggy dog ran directly to Meghan and lay down at her feet. Meghan introduced Nancy Davis, but then immediately began questioning Rebecca about her soil samples. The older woman answered in detail. She explained to Elizabeth that Meghan was a medical doctor with a professional interest in Hanford and its effects on nearby residents.

Meghan idly scratched Panda's head. "I grew up just over the state line in Oregon. Sheepherding country, wide-open spaces, the music of the spheres, and all that. But my thyroid quit working when I was in junior high. Have to take a pill every day to make up for it. Like a lot of kids growing up downwind of this place, my life has been changed by Hanford."

Elizabeth expressed mild surprise that someone harmed by Hanford would choose to live so near it.

"She's cursed with a conscience as strict as your own," said Rebecca to her old friend. "Quakers don't have a monopoly on virtue!"

"There's no virtue involved," Meghan interjected before Elizabeth could respond. "It really is a bit strange that anyone with a choice would be here, I agree. But I went away for college and medical school, and I guess I got through the first several stages of rage while I was gone. Ended up with a particular interest in certain radiation-related diseases. Between that and my family connections, my path led back here." With an ironic grin she added, "Right back here to the heart of darkness." In a more challenging tone she concluded, "And the same for you, Reba, even if it's at a later stage of life."

"We got to know each other through one of my mother's

Downwinder groups," Rebecca explained to Elizabeth. "We sort of egg each other on." Elizabeth nodded. "Come to the kitchen, all of you," added Rebecca in the clear tones of an administrator used to being in charge.

The four women, with Panda dogging Meghan's heels, trooped into the next room. Elizabeth felt her pulse quicken at the sense of energy and purpose these different women displayed. She kept a wary eye on the large, shaggy dog, but he stayed within a step of his mistress and had interest only in her.

Rebecca had spread out several maps and a stack of papers on the kitchen table. From the bottom of a satchel she produced what looked like a tulip planter, with a handle that screwed into threads just behind the spadelike implement.

"An official sampler of soil," she explained. "Dr. Bloch gave it to me. He says it takes a standard sample, up to the depth of this tube, you see. He even took me outside and showed me how to use it. And I've got some Baggies here, and a permanent pen to mark them."

"I'm sure that's all important," offered Nancy, the nurse. "Taking proper samples is the first step toward scientifically meaningful results."

"I love it!" exclaimed Meghan. "You're a closet techno-geek, Reba, just wasted in banking all those years!"

"Perhaps," Rebecca laughed. "Let me show all of you what I've been planning the last couple of months. This map covers my family's property. You can see Hanford's border here along the edge of the paper."

"It still amazes me that you don't glow in the dark, Reba,"

said Meghan, studying the map. "Growing up literally on Hanford's border!"

"Where exactly is this house?" asked Elizabeth, eager to understand all she could.

"It's here in the southwest corner," answered Rebecca, pointing to a box-shaped symbol. "What I've done so far, you see, is just take soil samples from within the boundaries of my property. They are marked here on the map as SS-one, SS-two, SS-three. I thought it seemed professional to call them 'soil sample one' and so on, you see. There are three samples, which I thought was quite a lot. But I've learned from Professor Bloch that what I had really isn't a large number. By his standards, they're all too close together and all from the topmost layer of the soil."

"I see," said Elizabeth, a bit unsure of herself.

"What's next?" asked Meghan briskly. Nancy nodded her interest.

"Two of my three samples," explained Rebecca, "counted as 'interesting' by Wenzel Bloch's standards. The feds are supposed to monitor such things, of course. And now, so is a state agency. But Professor Bloch says two of my samples show much higher values than anything that's been reported by the federal boys or by the state. So I'm going to try to get enough samples to be more than just 'interesting'—more like 'conclusive.' This time, I'll take a lot more samples, all across my property. And I might as well go onto the parts of the site that are open and sample the soils there, too."

Elizabeth instantly thought of her arthritic shoulders and

hoped she would not be asked to help with the manual labor. Then she sighed with self-reproach for her selfishness.

"This professor in Seattle will analyze everything for you?" asked Nancy skeptically.

"That's what he says. He's an old guy, and I guess this will be his last project. He says he'll get the funds for the laboratory work by robbing Peter to pay Paul. And, just to round things off, I'm also going to take water samples from the house here, and from all the neighbors who will let me," concluded Rebecca. "I've got special bottles to put the water in, superclean or something, from the university. Professor Bloch thinks the water may be more indicative of various things than the soil. But a number of houses will have to be sampled to be meaningful."

"We each have wells, you see," Meghan explained to Elizabeth. "Here in the country there's no water from the city system. The wells don't go down too deep, and it's sure possible they've been affected."

Rebecca sat down and motioned for the other three women to do the same. She looked thoughtfully at her Quaker friend. "I'll also try to get onto Hanford's restricted property, behind the big fences around the nuclear plants, and take some soil samples at the real sources themselves. But if I can't get permission, I won't ask you to trespass with me, Elizabeth, so don't worry."

"Actually," Elizabeth responded slowly, "trespassing is not so distressing as this whole notion of not trusting what the government has told you. The feds, as you call them, are trying to clean up Hanford now, aren't they? Would the government lie about your own soil and water?"

Rebecca shook her head in chagrin at her friend's innocence as Meghan jumped in.

"You don't know what's happened here, Mrs. Elliot. It's tough to take it in all at once, I'm sure. And even for us, the more we find out about what was done in the fifties and sixties, the more unreal it all seems."

"I don't like to think about it," Nancy said, "and maybe you know I work at the site. But it was just recently that the government released papers showing how much plutonium they had 'lost' in those two decades. It sounds incredible, but at one point they couldn't account for half a ton of it."

Meghan nodded her head emphatically, breaking into her friend's narrative. "The federal boys never did find that plutonium. Apparently it went up the smokestacks, getting around filters that were supposed to trap it. Plutonium is terribly lethal, even in trace amounts. Spreading half a ton of it around the region must have done a lot to increase cancer rates. We know this is hard to believe, but you can read about all this stuff in the papers. None of it is speculation; it's from the government's own records and reports. The Freedom of Information Act has brought it all to light at last."

"I do know that evil can be difficult to grasp," said Elizabeth somberly. "That's one way it tries to fool us."

"You could say that," responded the young doctor briskly, clearly not caring to consider the broader implications of thinking of evil as an embodied force. "Let me just sketch Hanford's history from the perspective of a Downwind kid like myself, OK?"

Elizabeth, effectively corralled, nodded.

"After making the plutonium for the Bomb," Meghan

began, "the guys who were running Hanford got used to thinking they were indispensable to the good ol' US of A. To keep ahead of the Russians, the Hanford boys tried to think up new and different nuclear weapons. They even tested one of their more basic ideas: they called it the 'Green Run.' "

"That experiment was not a high point in our nation's history," Rebecca interjected dryly.

Nancy simply looked away, apparently too pained by the topic to remain in eye contact.

"Everything connected with war becomes more and more terrible," agreed Elizabeth automatically. The lifelong pacifist added, without emotion, "That's the nature of violence."

"But get this!" Meghan broke in, eager to resume her narrative. "Hanford's engineers *deliberately* released large quantities of radiation up their smokestacks during the Green Run. They were thinking about a weapon that involved a cloud of radioactive material that would float over the USSR, see? Because nobody knew how long radioactive particles would stay in the air, and how far they would drift, and how much they would affect people, the Green Run tested the idea. But everything about it was secret—nobody living near here knew what the government was doing! So, during the test, invisible radioactive clouds were released here at Hanford, and they blew downwind. When it was all over, the boys working for Hanford went out and cataloged the effects of their experiment. They asked us locals how many of our farm animals had died."

"We just don't know," interjected Rebecca, "how many people were affected. Not right then, I mean, but in the years that followed when cancers would have been developing."

Elizabeth shook her head mutely, accepting what she was told.

"You can imagine," continued Meghan, "a place as out of control as Hanford in those days didn't just screw up once. There were many times that stupid decisions and sloppiness and bad luck got covered up. Leaking waste tanks and accidental explosions on the grounds of Hanford that killed workers and spread radiation—all of that happened and got hushed up."

"When a few brave people did come forward with parts of the true story," Rebecca interjected, "they were vilified."

Meghan was nodding her head and using both hands to punch the air. "Some of the whistle-blowers really suffered. People's constitutional rights got trampled underfoot. Most folks figured nobody could stand up to Hanford. It was the only big employer for hundreds of miles around here."

Nancy finally returned her gaze to the other women and broke into the conversation, saying, "People really thought Hanford was defending democracy and motherhood and apple pie against everything that those communists could do. And maybe it was. The Bomb, after all, kept the Soviet Union contained until it collapsed."

"That's right," said the doctor. "But that doesn't excuse the excesses, the willful contamination of land and water, the out-and-out deceit that went on for decades."

Everyone at the table nodded as Meghan's arms finally dropped to her side. In a moment, Panda's furry nose pushed itself under one of his mistress's hands.

"Argh!" cried Meghan, scratching Panda behind the ears with one hand and looking at her wristwatch on the other.

"I've got to run! The clinic is open this evening, and I'm on duty. Sorry, but we've got to really fly!"

With that, Meghan and Nancy made hasty good-byes. Panda ran easily at his mistress's heels as the two young women disappeared out the front door of the old farmhouse. In half a moment, the low growl of a pickup truck's engine coming to life drifted into the kitchen.

Rebecca smiled at her old friend. "Young people are enough to make a person dizzy."

Elizabeth could only agree.

"But it's time for us to eat," said Rebecca. She scooted her papers together in a heap. "We'll go meet my relatives and have some supper. Pamela, my cousin's wife, is a strict Baptist, so there won't be wine. But that's agreeable with you, as I recall."

"Indeed," answered the old Quaker.

The two women gathered up their heavy sweaters and went out the front door. Rebecca did not take the time to wrestle with the difficult lock, explaining that burglaries in central Washington State were not a big problem.

"My cousin, Lincoln Wilkinson, lives just two miles from here, down toward the throbbing metropolis of Benton City," she told her friend. "It'll only take a moment to get there."

"Considering how impressed you are with the environmental problems here," Elizabeth responded, "I'm a little surprised you not only visit here but eat and drink as well. Does that seem safe to you?"

Rebecca laughed. "You go from trusting the government, just because it's the government, to thinking we should leave for Seattle, all in twenty minutes!"

"Perhaps I'm easily swayed," answered Elizabeth without distress.

"Believe me," said Rebecca, "I would never spend more than a few days here. I'd like never to come here again, to sell the house and the land and be done with it. But it seems immoral to sell this old place, or even give it away, to some sucker who will live here year-round. Somebody who's likely to understand even less than I do about the radioactivity problems."

"How do your relatives here feel?"

"They desperately want to believe the government," answered Rebecca in a serious tone. "They're not like Meghan, my mother, and me. Most people right near Hanford aren't—they've got to fall asleep at night, you see, and it's easier to do that if you just deny all that's happened.

"Still, maybe even my cousins are now accepting Hanford's history for what it is. At least, when I was here last, Pam said something to me about selling their place and moving to Portland next spring. Lincoln is on disability—a bad back—and Pamela works from their home, selling Amway and Avon. So they're free to move before the heat hits next summer.

"I said I thought that going to Portland sounded wise, although to tell you the truth, it probably doesn't matter at this point. It's just too late for them." Rebecca pulled off the narrow but paved road and drove on a small gravel track toward a trailer home. "I'm not being hard-hearted, Elizabeth. It's just that my relatives have pretty well been exposed to all the stuff that's drifted around here, whatever it may have been. And so has their son. They had a daughter, by the way, but she died around 1980 from a rare type of brain malignancy. That's a subject well worth staying away from; it still makes Pam break down. Of course, not discussing what may have triggered that poor girl's illness is one way of coping with Hanford."

"Yes," said Elizabeth quietly. "Denial works well—for as long as a person can stick with it."

4

❦

I also saw that there was an ocean of darkness and death, but an infinite ocean of light and love, which flowed over the ocean of darkness. And in that also I saw the infinite love of God . . .

George Fox
Seventeenth-Century English Friend

In keeping with what seemed to be local habit, Elizabeth did not lock her door as she and her friend got out of the car after pulling up the gravel drive. The car looked small next to a large truck near the trailer.

"That's Lincoln's current pickup," said Rebecca, following Elizabeth's glance. "It's big, isn't it?"

The New Englander nodded.

"It's a three-fifty. Rather pretentious, actually."

Elizabeth frowned her lack of understanding.

"Do I have to explain everything?" laughed Rebecca. "Full-size Ford pickups all have the same body. But there are three engine sizes. One-fifty, two-fifty, and three-fifty. A three-fifty like this could haul a house down the road. Since the accident that wrecked Lincoln's back and landed him on disability, it's important to him to have a powerful truck—you know, a clear macho symbol."

"What's that?" asked Elizabeth, nodding toward the pickup's cab. A thick dark slash across the rear window had caught her eye.

"What, the gun rack?" asked Rebecca, genuinely confused.

"That's what it is?" asked the old Quaker rhetorically. She added, "Why does your cousin need a gun?"

"Well, a rifle or two, and a shotgun, are just standard equipment on any self-respecting pickup truck." Rebecca smiled at her friend. "Seriously, the guns aren't for a macho effect. They're quite utilitarian. Linc needs his weapons for the various seasons—hunting seasons. Game is probably his household's largest single source of protein. My cousin and cousin-in-law, you see, are hard up; they always have been." She squinted toward the Ford, then added, "It looks like he's carrying a semiautomatic rifle at the moment. I suppose it's for the deer season, and some men hunt elk around here. There's a group of elk that wandered onto Hanford long ago. The herd has grown now, and it's tempting to hunters, although hunting on the site is illegal—and stupid, since it might well provide the hunter with radioactive game for his table."

The two women turned toward the home in front of them just as they heard the words "Welcome, Reba!"

A cheerful, wiry woman of about sixty was walking briskly toward them. She hugged Rebecca and was introduced to Elizabeth. The New Englander wished she had changed into fresh clothes, particularly since Pamela was wearing a simple but neatly pressed printed dress.

"I'm glad you could come," said Pamela, smiling broadly and motioning them both toward the front door of her trailer home. "This place is not exactly a Best Western, but we're glad to have you."

Pamela looked like a strong woman, with unusually square shoulders and natural grace. Elizabeth immediately liked her ready smile and cheerful voice. Inside, Rebecca greeted her cousin, Lincoln, who rose from his reclining chair as the women entered. He was a red beet of a man, stocky and without his wife's ease of movement. He smiled thinly, as if in pain.

"It's good to see you all again!" Rebecca declared.

Elizabeth was not sure that the pleasure was reciprocated in Lincoln's case.

"This is new, isn't it?" asked Rebecca, waving her hand around the room.

"Yup," answered Lincoln with a bit more cheer, "all new. I got a terrific deal from a mobile-home guy, just by waiting, waiting, waiting, you know, till the time was right. We not only got the double-wide, set up here for free, but a written guarantee that they'll move it to Portland next spring."

"They'll move it," said Pamela cautiously, "but we'll have to pay a setup fee down there, I'm sure."

Elizabeth silently guessed that Pamela worried about details, while her husband liked to think he was a man of action. That, of course, was a common pattern in marriages, particularly in her generation.

"Do you have a trailer park picked out?" asked Rebecca agreeably.

"Yeah," Lincoln answered. "It's a nice little place, reserved for seniors. Very neat. And none of our scorching summers, of course. The rental for the space isn't bad, nothing worse than you'd pay in Richland."

"Supper won't be a moment, whether that boy of ours shows up or not," called Pamela and stepped into the kitchen.

"Tom is still at work at the site," explained Lincoln, "but he should be here any minute."

The two cousins exchanged small talk about the weather, the condition of the pass over the Cascade Mountains, and the increasingly sophisticated gambling available to citizens on Indian reservations throughout the state. Elizabeth noted that a tiny tic sometimes made Lincoln look as if he was wincing when he spoke. As the two talked, Elizabeth simply listened, and Pamela brought out bowl after bowl of steaming food to the table. It would have been better, the Quaker reproached herself, to help the hostess, but the kitchen was completely unfamiliar, and, in truth, she was deeply tired from traveling.

Just then a young man entered the small home, immediately kneeling down to remove filthy boots.

"Hi, Aunt Becky," he said politely. He then looked at his father and said in a deeper tone, "Another day, another dollar."

"Not a bad shift, I hope," said Lincoln.

"No, the usual stuff, really."

Tom smiled shyly at Elizabeth, realizing for the first time that there was a stranger in the room, and the two of them were introduced.

"Do you work at Hanford?" asked Elizabeth, simply out of politeness.

"Yeah," replied Tom, wiggling his toes inside his socks and

looking hopefully toward the dinner table. "I'm in Maintenance, for the motor pool."

"That's at Central Stores," interjected Rebecca, "almost in downtown Richland. It's quite a ways from here. Meghan's medical clinic is about halfway in between."

Elizabeth only dimly understood the geography of the region, but she nodded helpfully. "Maintaining automobiles is a real art," she said sincerely.

"My boy can fix any American-made vehicle," said Lincoln with the first real touch of warmth Elizabeth had yet seen in him. "No matter what the trouble is. He's a genius at the internal combustion engine."

"That's a great accomplishment," said Elizabeth quickly. "I've never understood cars in the slightest, even though I've been dealing with them for forty-five years."

"What do you own?" asked Tom.

"Don't laugh!" responded Elizabeth. "A '77 Chevrolet. Just before I left Cambridge I was told I needed new brakes and a new radiator. I guess it's time to turn in that car."

"No," said Tom, "maybe not. It's almost always worth fixing a car if the body is sound. I'm sure you get plenty of rain in the East, and in the winter you put salt down on your roads, don't you? What's the rust like underneath your Chevy?"

A rather lengthy discussion followed that began with Elizabeth's car and progressed to the relative merits of other American-made sedans. Tom seemed well informed and evenhanded in his opinions, but his father had uniformly harsh words for all recent models. By the time the automobile conversation had run its course, all five people were midway through the pot roast and potatoes that Pamela had served. The only interruption had been for a brief prayer hurriedly said by Lincoln before they began to eat.

At the end of the meal Lincoln turned to Rebecca. He asked in a suddenly weary tone, "Have you come back here for more of those samples of yours?"

"That's right," said Rebecca in a businesslike voice. "I'll collect as many as I can around here in the next few days and take them back to the University of Washington. I've got a professional gadget with me that will allow me to get down deeper into the soil and take a proper sample. And I'm going to get water samples, too, from the private wells all around here."

Elizabeth watched Pamela as she looked at her husband with evident distress.

"Do you think it's really needed?" asked Pamela softly, turning her gaze toward Rebecca.

"Absolutely!" responded her cousin-in-law. "The government hasn't told us the truth up till now, has it? It's time we Downwinders had some concrete information of our own."

"I don't think you should be poking your nose into this," said Lincoln angrily. "You don't even live here. It's not you and yours that are at stake."

"Cousin, I count you as part of me and mine," answered Rebecca, "and although I may not live here, I now own a lot of acreage just north of this town. I'd be glad to sell my property, but I'm not going to unload something that would put more people at risk if they lived here."

"I've always daydreamed that I might come into your land,

Aunt," said Tom easily. "Seeing I'm your only relative in the next generation."

"Sorry," said Rebecca. "That would be a fine idea, but I've willed the cash value of my estate, such as it is, to a few favorite charities in Seattle. The will isn't going to change."

Both Tom and Rebecca had spoken in a low-key manner, and Elizabeth thought both were relaxed about the subject of Rebecca's assets. Indeed, it seemed the information was not new to anyone at the table.

But Lincoln was evidently distressed by something else.

"You see!" he spat out. "It's always Seattle this, Seattle that. Reba, you don't think about those of us who live here. Taking samples and mucking around the site just doesn't make sense. Keep your conscience on the wet side of the state, why don't you!"

"Lincoln!" interjected Pamela. She smiled weakly at Elizabeth and tried to apologize to Rebecca.

Lincoln sat, brooding, as Tom silently cleared his plate of dessert. Pamela turned the conversation to another cousin, a lawyer in Idaho, and the tension slowly eased. Elizabeth, who knew that relatives often could not discuss subjects about which they seriously disagreed, was glad she was not a part of the argument. Mercifully, and apparently to no one's surprise, the night wound up early. Rebecca and Elizabeth departed the trailer, satiated with meat and carbohydrates and ready for a good night's rest.

They stepped out under a clear night sky. With Pamela calling good-bye after them, they walked toward their car in the dense darkness of a rural night. But above them, Elizabeth saw thousands of stars splashed across a coal-black sky.

"So many stars," she mused seriously. "A night like this gives me a sense of the immediacy of God's creation." She smiled upward, then added, "Almost none of these stars is visible in Cambridge."

"That's the trouble with life in Boston," agreed her old friend. "A person living there can't see what's important. But," she added easily, "Seattle is no better."

The two women drove slowly through the night toward Rebecca's childhood home.

5

❦

. . . the ocean of Light of which Fox and other writers speak so movingly does not simply roll in and cover the ocean of evil, violence, hatred, and selfishness. On the contrary . . . it is enriched, even transformed, by a recognition of the darkness . . . we are citizens of two Kingdoms—the Kingdom of Light and the Kingdom of Darkness, and the highest citizenship of all, the allegiance beyond all others, brings with it passports to them both.

Helen Hole
Twentieth-Century American Friend

Morning dawned clear and cold. The wind was blowing strongly from the west when Elizabeth awoke in the chilly back bedroom of the Nichols family house. She dressed quickly in the same slacks she had worn the previous day. It wasn't that she particularly liked them, nor certainly the state they were in, but she anticipated she would be outside all day, helping her old friend with soil samples. Dressed for such work, Elizabeth went stiffly but determinedly down the stairs to the first floor.

Rebecca was already up, and a pot of coffee was on the stove. Elizabeth was grateful that it was much warmer in the kitchen than it had been in her room. Rebecca produced breakfast within a few minutes, drawing on the supplies from an ice chest she had brought in her car trunk from Seattle.

"I don't like to buy milk around here," she explained, "knowing what might be in it. It's one thing to eat Pam's pot roast, from cattle probably raised in Argentina, but it's another thing to use dairy products that are much more local. But as Lincoln would say, that's a Seattle perspective."

After breakfasting and cleaning up, the two women put on their coats and hats, gathered up their gear, and went out to Rebecca's car.

"We'll start on my property first, taking proper samples this time," explained Rebecca. "We can drive on the dirt road behind the house over to the border between my land and Hanford."

The next two hours were spent walking on the Nichols family's property, along Hanford's southern border. Rebecca took samples, putting the soil in Baggies and giving them a number. Each time, after digging, she scraped loose dirt together and tamped it down into the hole she had made. This attempt to disturb the land as little as possible was something Elizabeth recognized from her Green friends in New England. For her part, Elizabeth marked the samples' locations and numbers on the map.

Elizabeth had plenty of time to marvel at the strange country around them. Sage, rocks, and barren patches of dirt lay under the beautiful, cobalt-blue sky that stretched in a sweeping arc over her head. But after a while, the absence of trees gave Elizabeth a desolate, almost desperate feeling. She began to tire as the sun climbed higher. Finally Rebecca said they were finished and should turn back to the car with their burdens.

Just then, Elizabeth screamed at a rattlesnake in front of her. She dropped the map and the pencil as she stumbled backward.

"Don't panic!" shouted Rebecca.

She came over to Elizabeth's side and put an arm around her friend's shoulders.

"That snake is dead. See how flat it is? It's been out here since last summer, and its insides have dried up."

Elizabeth shook her head, still afraid.

"This is October, Elizabeth," continued Rebecca in a soothing tone, "and it's cold out here. That means we won't meet active rattlers. They're deep in their holes somewhere, keeping warm. Maybe listening to the morning news."

Shaken still, but finally able to function, Elizabeth gathered up the things she had dropped.

"Sorry," she said. "I'm just not used to the idea of poisonous snakes underfoot. Bees are the most dangerous creatures we have in New England."

"Come back to the car and we'll put these samples in the trunk," Rebecca directed. "I've got a thermos of tea for you."

After sweetened tea, drunk inside the sun-warmed Saab, Elizabeth felt restored. She smiled and indicated she was ready for more.

"That's my roomie!" responded Rebecca. Evidently she had only been waiting for a signal from Elizabeth, and her plans were well in place. "Here's what we'll do: we've been at the very edge of my property, just a few yards from what is officially Hanford. But the site is huge, about a quarter the size of all of Massachusetts. The parts of it that are really contaminated are near the nuclear plants. They're up by the Columbia River.

"I want you to see how gorgeous this part of the Northwest can be, Elizabeth. So we'll drive most of the way across the site, to its border in the north. The Columbia up there is magnificent."

Elizabeth politely agreed, and the two drove on the narrow dirt track to the blacktop highway. From there they turned north. At first Elizabeth could not tell whether or not they were on government property. The desert around them was just the same, the road still narrow but well maintained. By New England standards, there was no traffic at all on the highway, which made their journey seem a bit eerie to Elizabeth.

Sensing her visitor's thoughts, Rebecca said, "It's quite different from what it was during the Cold War. In those days, a person couldn't just drive onto Hanford. The whole place was off-limits to normal citizens like us. Really off-limits: even commercial airplanes couldn't fly over the site. There were antiaircraft guns over there"—she waved to the Rattlesnake Hills on her left—"to enforce the no-fly zone. Likewise, no boats could go up the Columbia from Richland, nor come down the upper part of the river into the Hanford Reach. For decades, there just was no access to any of this. Now, by comparison, there's a great deal of freedom.

"I'll show you something amusing," said Rebecca abruptly. She braked and turned off the road to the left, following another piece of blacktop up a long, low hill. She stopped the car at a locked gate that stretched across the pavement.

"Care to read the signs?" she asked.

Elizabeth had already begun to do so. There were two, the first of which read:

NATIONAL ECOLOGICAL RESEARCH SITE

U.S. DEPARTMENT OF ENERGY

"That's the new name for several pieces of Hanford," explained Rebecca. "Ecology sounds so much better than nuclear waste, don't you think?"

A second sign was mounted near the bottom of a tall pole. It read:

> CAUTION:
> IF SIREN SOUNDS, EVACUATE THE ENTIRE AREA
> IMMEDIATELY. TUNE YOUR RADIO TO AM 530
> FOR EMERGENCY INFORMATION.

Solar panels on the ground led to wires that went up to the top of the pole, where a large siren was mounted.

"Not all ecological research sites have to warn people about explosions," said Rebecca dryly, turning her car in front of the gate.

Around them, the empty desert stretched in every direction.

"It's surreal," Elizabeth offered simply.

"That it is," responded Rebecca with a nod. "For decades, by the way, Hanford wasn't on any maps. Nothing was marked. This place was just an empty space! And even today, the map that Richland's Chamber of Commerce prints doesn't show Hanford at all. It's tough to know how to respond to Big Brother when he can so easily pretend that he's really studying ecology—or that he doesn't even exist!"

They quickly returned to the main road and continued north. They met no guards or checkpoints, but simply continued onward as if the road were a perfectly normal one.

"I won't explain all the smokestacks you can see toward

the eastern horizon, Elizabeth," said Rebecca. "Let's not think about all that until we've seen something good about Hanford."

"I'm glad if there can be anything positive about this place," said Elizabeth sincerely.

"There is one great thing: the Columbia River, free-flowing for miles and miles! The northern part of Hanford contains the only part of the river that still flows down-stream. All the rest of it, from the Pacific Ocean to Canada, has been dammed up by the feds, specifically the Corps of Engineers."

Rebecca continued to talk, trying to describe to Elizabeth what all the rivers in the Northwest had been like in her childhood. Before the dams were erected, the Columbia and its tributaries had been cold, clear rivers, glistening with trout and salmon. Rebecca related the spirit of fishing expeditions she had enjoyed as a small child, and tried to explain the dependence of the local Indians on what the rivers of the area used to yield.

Eventually, Rebecca's sleek car topped the edge of a huge ridge, and the Columbia River came into view. The road swooped down toward the water, and Rebecca allowed the car to accelerate under the force of gravity.

"Everything in the Northwest seems built on such a big scale," said Elizabeth appreciatively, taking in the vista. As they neared the river, she saw the sun glinting off the water's undulating surface. The river looked to Elizabeth like a miracle, albeit a narrow one. A fine but oddly empty bridge was built across the Columbia. The pilings of the bridge each carved a white plume into the river's surface, clear testimony to the water's strong current towards the east.

"This is Vernita Bridge," explained Rebecca, stopping the car just at the start of the bridge. "For miles and miles below here the river flows unimpeded. We call this the Hanford Reach. This area is a favorite of migratory birds. And it's good for salmon, too. There are more eagles here, fishing for salmon, than anywhere else in the Northwest. The radioactive leaks may have poisoned a few generations of wildlife, but they've recovered now." She swept her eyes across the broad and bare hills and downstream along the river. "Salmon and wild geese and eagles! All of that, just from letting the water flow downhill like the good Lord intended!"

Elizabeth nodded silently.

Rebecca got out of the car, and Elizabeth did the same, although much more slowly.

"I'm sorry to be dim," Elizabeth said as they stood looking at the austere grandeur around them, "but I don't understand why this part of the Columbia wasn't touched when all the rest of its length was dammed up."

"Because of the nukes themselves, that's all," responded Rebecca. "Remember the timing of the war, Elizabeth. The nuclear reactors on the site, you see, were built before all the dams. Well, except for Grand Coulee."

"Which is in Washington?" asked Elizabeth uncertainly.

"Yes," laughed Rebecca. "Of course it is! But it's upriver toward Canada, a long way from here. Anyway, after the war, the Corps of Engineers started building dams all over the place. But dams always flood the banks of a river, and all its tributaries, right? You see, not even the Corps could flood anything as important as our nation's sole source of plutonium. So from here all across the site to the city of Richland, the Columbia is still running free. As you were saying a while back, it's all a tad surreal."

Rebecca stretched her arms over her head and breathed deeply with evident pleasure. Standing normally once again, she smiled at her old friend, and asked if Elizabeth could see the coyote across the river from them. Startled, the Quaker looked carefully where her friend pointed and saw a scrawny, gray-brown creature loping along the bank.

"When I was a child," explained Rebecca, "you hardly saw a coyote. You could hear them at night, of course, but they were awfully shy of humans. These days, though, they're quite brazen. They even come into Benton City, scavenging in garbage cans and eating the occasional cat."

"Oh," said Elizabeth in dismay. Her thoughts raced back to Cambridge and to Sparkle.

The coyote disappeared into the sagebrush, and Rebecca asked if Elizabeth was ready to get back to more serious tasks. They turned the car around, but left the bridge on a different road from that on which they had come. It was a narrow gravel track through the desert, and dead ahead Elizabeth could not help but see enormous buildings and smokestacks on the horizon.

"We're basically following the Columbia downstream," explained Rebecca. "The river runs in a straight line for a while here, so it will keep us company. What you see ahead is called One Hundred B and C Areas. That's Hanfordspeak for one of the original sites of the nuclear reactors that made plutonium. They used water from the Columbia, you see, to cool the reactor cores. That's why they wanted to be so close to the river.

"I'm choosing this place for some more samples just because it's so near the public-access part of Hanford. This is just a little back road, and I think it won't be actively guarded. I imagine I'll be able to drive right up to the big fence that's around those buildings. I want soil samples from one of the really nasty places, you see, for Professor Bloch. He'll do the work to see what's really in the top layer of soil these days, and how that compares to what's just outside the site."

"Such as your property?"

"Exactly. Radioactive particles of any kind that are loose on the desert floor are going to end up being blown around. We have real windstorms here sometimes, Elizabeth, and without much vegetation to hold anything in place, the dust gets picked up and moved for miles. What's up here at B Plant—I mean what's in the top layer of the soil—will certainly be blown into the Columbia, or around the site, or over to Richland or Benton City. It just depends which way the wind is coming from on a particular day."

Elizabeth studied the improbably huge buildings drawing nearer and nearer. Dozens of dark power lines led across the desert, looking like long tentacles of some giant malignancy. She felt her abdomen tighten into a heavy knot, a familiar response to anything her heart felt was entirely contrary to the will of God. Soon the old Quaker could see a chain-link fence surrounding the buildings. She was relieved, trusting that the fence would prevent them from getting too near to what she could only think of as a thoroughly evil place. But she didn't understand the unusual silhouette made by one section of the fence, and she asked Rebecca what accounted for it.

"You'll see when we get closer," answered her friend. "It's just tumbleweeds blown up against the chain links. Here in the dry part of the state, our fences always end up with botanical decoration."

Elizabeth nodded her understanding.

"The tumbleweed has been a bit of a health problem," added Rebecca. "The plants here on the site pick up radioactive particles in the soil and groundwater as they grow. Then when they die and start being blown around, they can travel for a hundred miles or more. So the tumbleweeds have actually spread radioactive material over to easternmost Washington and Oregon."

A locked gate blocked their progress at the fence. Rebecca simply turned off the engine, leaving the car in the center of the narrow gravel road on which they had come. There had been no sign of another human being since they had left the bridge over the Columbia.

"OK," announced Rebecca. "I want to take samples up and down this fence. You'll find this place on the map, Elizabeth. Just look for the B Plant and the westernmost fence around it."

Elizabeth was unhappy with what she thought of as technical—if not aggressive—trespassing, and she was weighed down with depression from the sight of the nuclear plant in front of her. Nevertheless, she realized that the only way they were going to be able to leave was to do what Rebecca wanted. She got out of the car, checking their location on the map as Rebecca started taking her first sample just a few feet off the road. The work continued for a long time, until fourteen samples along the fence had been collected, labeled, and marked on the map. Rebecca faithfully filled each hole she made, stamping the friable desert soil down with her foot.

"Whew!" said Rebecca. "My arms are starting to ache. I couldn't make any progress at all, I'm sure, except that it rained a lot a week ago. That loosened up the soil, or what passes for soil around here. But still, this isn't the easiest of work!"

"Especially not in one's retirement," observed Elizabeth dryly.

"Maybe you're drawing your Social Security, but I'm not," laughed Rebecca. "There's just one more set of samples I want to get."

"Not another long drive," Elizabeth moaned involuntarily. She was genuinely exhausted, more from emotional stress than from the minimal work she had done.

"No drive required!" announced Rebecca, marching off into the desert. "And when we're done, I'll take you to Richland's best restaurant for lunch."

"Where are you going?" called Elizabeth.

Rebecca made no reply, and with a sigh the Quaker slowly followed her friend around a clump of sagebrush. Although Elizabeth walked with difficulty, she was determined, and in time she came to the top of a rise, where Rebecca was waiting for her.

Pointing down, further into the desert, Rebecca said, "See?

At the bottom of that little gully, there's a serious hole in the B Plant's fence. I'm going to make use of it."

Elizabeth shook her head vigorously, too concerned to immediately find the words she wanted.

"You don't have to come with me," said Rebecca. "Just stand here and watch me through the fence. I'll walk across the big hill there, and when I take a sample I'll wave at you and you can mark it on the map. Is that OK with your Quaker conscience?"

Elizabeth hesitated, then answered quietly, "It always takes a long time for me to make up my mind about any moral question. I'm not an executive like you, making big judgments each and every moment. Since you're asking my thoughts, I would certainly prefer it if you'd get the government's permission for taking samples on its property."

"Elizabeth, don't be naive!"

Elizabeth considered her options and decided they were few.

"I'll stand here and mark places on the map," she finally said.

"Good girl!" cried Rebecca with delight. "Please forgive my pushing you, if you can. I'm pretty wrapped up in all of this, I know, but you can imagine how it might feel if you had grown up here. Every bone in my body feels at home near the Columbia." Her voiced warmed with emotion as she spoke. "Look at that sky to the west! Can you see Mount Adams, almost floating on the horizon?"

Elizabeth could, indeed, see a distant but spectacular snowcapped peak in the direction Rebecca was pointing.

"This is God's country, Elizabeth! Or it was. Look east, and you see these hideous, hulking plutonium plants. The feds have poisoned my home, the best home a person could have. I know there's no changing the past. But the government hasn't admitted to all the harm they've done to the residents and the land here. We can help change that part of the story."

"You can, Rebecca. I'm just here on a visit," replied Elizabeth quickly.

Rebecca made it to the base of the gully, and then got down on all fours and slowly squeezed through the gap. Elizabeth marveled at her friend's flexibility, and fought off a moment of envy as she watched. Rebecca, for her part, dusted herself off, then turned and walked up the broad ridge sloping to the north behind the fence. A third of the way up the hill, she turned and waved at Elizabeth, then bent over to the dirt.

Elizabeth struggled to open the map in the breeze, found her place, and made a mark on the map. It was unfortunate they had not agreed on a numbering system for this next batch of samples. After some thought she wrote down "SUR 1" on the map, which in her mind stood for "surreptitious sample number one." By the time she had finished her deliberations and written the code, Rebecca was walking up the hill again.

Just then, a jeep with a large automatic gun mounted on its hood came around the edge of the hill, moving fast. Elizabeth almost cursed herself, both for her stupidity in going along with Rebecca's plan and her cowardliness in staying on the relatively safe side of the fence. The jeep changed course and rapidly overtook Rebecca, who had stopped to watch it come up to her.

Elizabeth became frantic. She debated in her mind going through the fence to be with her friend, or staying where she was. On the outside of the fence, she decided, she would be providing one witness to anything that might happen. She realized with a start that such a thought tended toward the paranoid. What Rebecca had been telling her about Hanford had apparently now deeply affected her outlook about this strange, bone-dry place.

There were two men in the jeep talking to Rebecca. They got out of their vehicle and then moved with her between them toward the hole in the fence. They were apparently walking in silence. Rebecca still held the sampling spade in one hand and several empty Baggies in the other. The group came up to the chain-link fence, draped here and there with tumbleweed.

"Make a note of this gap, Al. I want it fixed before you go home today," said the man leading the way.

"Yes, sir," grunted his companion. By Elizabeth's estimate, he must have weighed well over two hundred pounds, each ounce well distributed across his massive frame. He came up to the fence and stooped to examine the hole, not looking at Elizabeth even though she was only a few feet away. He wore a uniform, and Elizabeth saw the name "Cartwright" printed above the breast pocket of his jacket.

"The keys are in the ignition," Rebecca called to Elizabeth. "Go back to my house. The telephone is turned off because the house has been closed up, but I'll call Meghan at her clinic when they release me."

"Oh, Rebecca!" said Elizabeth pointlessly.

"What's your name?" asked the man evidently in charge, looking Elizabeth up and down.

"You don't have to answer that!" barked Rebecca.

"Take her to the jeep!" ordered the senior security man to Cartwright.

The big man easily herded the defiant Miss Nichols in the direction of the vehicle.

"What's your name?" repeated the man left standing at the fence.

"Elizabeth Elliot," replied the Quaker. She saw no reason not to give anyone this piece of information.

"You've been aiding and abetting," he barked. "If I see you again, I'll take you in, just like your friend here."

"I'm sure you could," answered Elizabeth steadily, acknowledging what she thought was both important and obvious.

"A smart-ass, eh?" answered the straw boss.

He turned on his heel and marched to the jeep. In just a moment, he drove over the brow of the low hill and out of sight, taking both his massive assistant and Rebecca Nichols with him.

6

Faith which overflows in real spiritual power must be fed with prayer.

Helen Hole
Twentieth-Century American Friend

Elizabeth stood for a few minutes at the fence after Rebecca and the jeep had disappeared. Her mind rushed from one fragmented idea to another. Finally, she silently shook her head and closed her eyes in an attempt to pray. Her thoughts continued to race ahead of her will, however, and she could not concentrate. Discouraged, she walked slowly to Rebecca's car.

As Elizabeth slid behind the automobile's steering wheel a verse from one of Paul's letters vibrated in the silent atmosphere of the small car:

> *My grace is sufficient for you;*
> *it is made perfect in your weakness.*

With a calm sense of mission, she put the car in gear, turned around, and drove back on the narrow gravel track. Coming out of the desert near the massive frame of Vernita Bridge, she got back on the paved road, heading south. After a long drive, she passed Rebecca's house but kept going, driving into the heart of Benton City.

The little town offered Elizabeth a combination gasoline station and bar, and although she did not like to be on premises devoted to alcohol consumption, she went inside. Here in the sparsely populated West, she reasoned, a Quaker must use what few human resources were available, however they might manifest themselves. While standing at the bar, she looked through a telephone book, finding the name and address of a medical clinic that listed Dr. M. K. Zillann on its roster. From the proprietor, she got directions to the clinic, which lay between Benton City and Richland. Within fifteen minutes, she had driven to the place.

The building was a small structure, one story high and made of cement blocks. Dusty pickup trucks, with strong lists betraying their ages, and old Chevy sedans filled the parking lot. House trailers of distinguished vintage but poor upkeep were scattered around the neighborhood, a place clearly not governed by the concept of zoning. Elizabeth, looking at both the humble clinic and its dreary surroundings, began to respect Meghan greatly.

As she crossed the parking lot and walked to the front entrance, the cautious Quaker directed her steps around a large dog dozing in the sun. As she passed him, he raised his head. It was, she realized, Meghan's sheepdog. She spoke his name, and the dog gave one thump of its tail in acknowledgment that they had met before. Elizabeth did not press for anything more but simply went inside.

Meghan's voice was the first she heard, although a moment later it was complemented by a baby's shrill wail.

"That's right, Rochelle," Meghan was saying, handing a baby to a remarkably young and painfully thin woman who stood in a hallway just off the crowded waiting room. "She needs this medicine three times a day. Give her these drops first thing in the morning, at noon, and last thing at night. Right? Three times every day."

Elizabeth saw Meghan break into an easy smile.

"She's a strong little thing, so don't be worried. Just bring her back on Monday, OK? And don't forget that you need to rest, too."

The girl named Rochelle tried to respond, but the protesting baby in her arms took all her attention. The young doctor, who was carrying the baby's bag of necessaries, escorted mother and child toward the front door, where she hooked the bag over Rochelle's shoulder and gave her a final few words of encouragement.

Catching sight of Elizabeth, Meghan stopped and looked perplexed. Noting the somber expression on the older woman's face, the doctor nodded to indicate they should follow Rochelle and her burdens outside. As they did so, Panda was instantly on his feet, nuzzling his mistress's hand.

"What's up, Mrs. Elliot?" said Meghan, ruffling the long coat of the sheepdog with one hand.

Elizabeth explained what had happened at the B Plant fence. "I don't know what to do," she concluded. "Since Rebecca said that she'd call here when she was released, I thought I'd like to wait at your clinic. I'll go pick her up when they set her free."

"Fine!" said Meghan readily, giving Panda one last scratch behind the ears. "Come on in. We'll put you to work, if you don't mind. There's always plenty to do around here! And as compensation I can promise a hurried lunch eaten in the middle of chaos." Meghan opened the door for Elizabeth with a flourish. "Seriously," she continued, "I was just going to order the staff something Mexican from the place down the road. They deliver. Are burritos OK with you?"

The afternoon went by in a blur. The take-out food proved too spicy for Elizabeth, but that hardly mattered since there was no time, at least by her standards, to eat it. The Quaker found herself filing charts, recording the weight of babies and the height of school-age children, and emptying the overflowing wastebaskets. At four o'clock Meghan appeared in the front office, took Elizabeth by the elbow, and steered her toward the door.

"No call from Reba yet. But at least I'm off now," she explained. "One of the good things about this clinic is that the MDs keep fairly regular hours. That's the advantage of having half a dozen of us."

Elizabeth expressed her appreciation of doctors who worked for the poor.

"We aren't saints," answered Meghan with a laugh as she opened the door for Elizabeth. Panda, hearing Meghan's voice, bounded up to them as they stepped onto the rough gravel of the parking lot. "Some of the docs are here because time spent in this clinic is counted as repayment of student loans. And some are here because they like general medicine—and a less than affluent clientele guarantees a doctor a wide range of conditions to treat. And some of us are here because keeping to regular hours lets us do some other things with our lives."

Panda leaped to the back of a dusty, full-size pickup at the end of the small lot. Meghan urged Elizabeth to ride with her and helped her get into the passenger side of the cab. It wasn't an easy maneuver for the arthritic old Quaker, in part because the truck was set unusually high off the ground by oversized, heavily lugged tires. But once she was inside, the truck was comfortable. With a growl from the big tires on the gravel, the pair exited onto the blacktop. As the vehicle was bouncing onto the street, it passed a white pickup truck parked immediately across from the parking lot exit. The white pickup was built on a smaller scale than Meghan's behemoth. Its engine was idling, the driver at the wheel. Elizabeth was startled to recognize the man named Al Cartwright whom she had seen a few hours earlier at the Hanford fence.

Well, she thought, *could this neighborhood be where he lives?* But she knew the odds were against that. Glancing back at the parking lot they had just left, Elizabeth was uncomfortably aware that Rebecca's small blue Saab stood out in this heartland of American-made vehicles.

And now, she said to herself with chagrin, *he's linked me to Meghan and this truck!*

But in a flash Elizabeth was reproaching herself for paranoia. This was, after all, the United States of America. She and Meghan had violated no law, and Rebecca's infringement on the law of trespass was surely a minor concern to the government.

"We'll just buzz over to the easiest part of Hanford to reach," Meghan was saying. "It's Central Stores, and Receiving, and all that. We'll ask about Rebecca there. Maybe the federal boys gave her a lift home, you know. That's the most likely thing, and then she couldn't call us, what with the telephone being off at her family's place. It's a considerable walk to her cousin's trailer or anything else in Benton City."

Meghan drove the big truck as if there were no speed limit. A breakneck pace, it seemed, was the young woman's habit. Elizabeth was not scared of an accident, for the huge roads and wide-open spaces of the West made crashes seem most unlikely. But hurrying to get to a place where they would surely arrive in any event was a clear sign, in her opinion, that they were not in control of what they were doing. "No one can add time to his life by hurrying" was an old Quaker expression Elizabeth cherished, and it was clearly at odds with the spirit of speeding.

"Downtown Richland is just a few blocks to our right now," Meghan announced presently, as the truck flew under a green highway sign marked HANFORD WORKS. "We'll turn onto government property here. This is the public center of the heart of darkness, if you will." Meghan pulled off at the largest building in the area, rolled down her window, and inquired of armed security men in a booth about Rebecca.

In the late afternoon gloom, the guards and the building marked CENTRAL STORES probably appeared more ominous to Elizabeth than they would have in brighter light. Even in the comfort and safety of Meghan's pickup, she felt oppressed by the heavy presence of institutionalized power all around her.

After a few minutes of conferring with their superiors by telephone, the two uniformed guards insisted that nobody like Rebecca Nichols was known to have been within Hanford at any time during the day.

"But she was on your property," protested Elizabeth, leaning over to speak across Meghan's lap to the open window. "She was at what I think is called B Plant. And she was taken away by two men in an official jeep. One of them was named Al Cartwright. You must check with him and his supervisor!"

Another telephone call by the man who was apparently the senior guard produced the same results.

"There's no information about this supposed person," he said sternly. "And that means she was never on the site. Not at any time today. Now turn this truck around."

"We know she was taken away by your security goons," said Meghan determinedly. "You can't just deny her existence."

"Turn your truck around. Clear this area or I'll take you both into custody!"

Meghan muttered words that made Elizabeth's ears sting as she put the big truck in gear. Looking through the back window of the cab, Elizabeth saw Panda, every inch of him alert, drinking in the scene around them.

Elizabeth could not keep a note of desperation out of her voice. "What can we do now?"

"Rebecca will turn up," said Meghan flatly, clearly willing it to be so as she rolled up her window. "Despite Hanford's long arms around here, the federal Constitution still means something, I think. Those bastards can't just hold a person and deny that they've got her."

She accelerated onto the highway, the engine actually torquing the cab under the demand placed on it.

"Sorry, I misspoke," said Meghan briskly. "After all, I shouldn't blame those men's mothers for them. They got where they are on their own." She rolled her head around her shoulders, apparently to ease inner tension. "As for us," she continued, "first we'll go to the Benton County sheriff's office and file a missing-person report. Then I'll call the ACLU. We don't have many civil-liberties types around here, as you can imagine, but I know they've got an office in Seattle."

Meghan turned almost shyly toward Elizabeth for a split second as she added, "Sometimes cities do have a few good things to offer." She concluded more firmly, "But I'll take life in the rural parts of the Northwest any day. Like we say, Seattle has been really Californicated."

Elizabeth was spared from having to make any reply by the abrupt appearance in front of them of a slow-moving flatbed truck. Meghan passed the obstacle with a controlled, precise movement, accelerating even as she pulled back into her lane. The unusually high cab of the pickup, Elizabeth realized, did give the driver the advantage of being able to see more of the road.

It was a considerable drive to the Benton County sheriff's office, located in the town of Prosser.

"This is where I took Nancy for her divorce papers yesterday," said Meghan. "Reba must have driven you right by here."

"I think I may have been asleep," responded Elizabeth. "Although the name Prosser does seem a little familiar."

At a stately, gray-stone courthouse in the middle of the older section of town, the two women found the sheriff's office. A deputy, lanky and blond with close-cropped hair, who looked to Elizabeth as if he belonged in high school, dutifully took down a description of Rebecca Nichols. But at the mention of Hanford he excused himself and returned with his boss.

Initially, Sheriff Tomlinson fit Elizabeth's stereotype of a rural law officer quite nicely. He was a big man. At six foot five, with shoulders seemingly broader than the interstate, he filled a good portion of the room. He had on a short, insulated jacket that hung open, showing his uniform shirt beneath. Just under the jacket, between his narrow waist and hips, hung a gun belt ringed with shells, and the holster it held up looked almost as large as the man who wore it.

To Elizabeth, everyone carrying a gun was a member of the violent, secular part of America with which no Friend could ever identify. But she soon realized that the man in front of her was not used to getting his way by brute strength. He introduced himself pleasantly in precisely enunciated English, sized up Elizabeth and Meghan in a glance—but with a smile as well—and asked what the problem was.

"Please start at the beginning," he added. "It will save time in the end. And economy, as we all know, is highly valued in government, even law enforcement, these days."

Taking the man at his word, Elizabeth told Sheriff Tomlinson of Rebecca's concern about contamination of her land from the Hanford site; about the possibility, now that her mother was dead, that she might sell her property if she thought it was not a health risk; and about the day's adventures taking soil samples. She described as best she could, the security men they had met, mentioning the large man named Al Cartwright and the other, seemingly superior person.

Having got that far, Elizabeth hesitated. She was unsure whether she should mention seeing Cartwright hours later, watching the blue Saab she'd parked at the medical clinic. She knew that part of the story might sound extremely unlikely to the sheriff, perhaps making him think that she and her friends were paranoid. In her moment of hesitation, Meghan jumped in with a recitation of the denials they'd been given at Hanford's main gate.

The sheriff nodded his understanding. He spoke a few words to the young deputy, and the boy, as Elizabeth thought of him, departed purposefully.

"This is not a missing-person case," explained the sheriff to Elizabeth, "if your friend is, in fact, sitting in her house right now waiting for you to return."

Meghan interjected, "But the goons wouldn't even admit they'd taken her into custody earlier today!"

The sheriff continued to focus on Elizabeth. "I've sent one of my deputies to check on the house. He'll radio in when he's been to the Nichols property."

Turning to Meghan, he added, "If we do have a true missing person, I'll be glad to take up the matter with the security team at the Hanford site."

Elizabeth thanked the sheriff, and the big man rose to his feet.

"You're welcome to wait here. The radio call will come through shortly, I'm sure. There's a coffeepot in the next room."

Meghan and Elizabeth availed themselves of a cup of bitter coffee and waited. Time passed slowly, and soon Elizabeth simply lost track of it. After what seemed to be a small eternity, Meghan stood up and announced her intention to speak to Panda, whom they had left in the bed of the pickup truck.

"He'll wait for as long as it takes," she explained to Elizabeth as she headed for the door. "But I'll encourage him, since it's getting close to his suppertime."

Meghan was gone only a couple of minutes. Just as she was returning, the physically imposing sheriff reappeared at Elizabeth's elbow.

"You'll both have to come with me to the Nichols property," he said briskly. "My deputy has discovered a woman's body—shot to death—outside the house." Carefully, indeed almost tenderly, he turned his whole concentration on Elizabeth as he continued more quietly. "From your description,

Mrs. Elliot, I think the woman may well be Rebecca Nichols. I'll ask you to do an official identification for us."

The drive to Rebecca's family homestead was a dark and confused blur to Elizabeth. The sun was touching the western horizon as they left the county courthouse, making the scene a mixture of burnt orange and the denser gloom of evening. Elizabeth rode with the sheriff, at his insistence, while Meghan was allowed to follow in her pickup. The county's official Crown Victoria roared to life with a power unexpected to the old Quaker, and they covered ground quickly and smoothly over the interstate. Although Meghan's truck was able to keep up, Elizabeth was sure even it was hard-pressed. She wondered how Panda was managing, loose in the bed of the truck.

How can I think of such things now? she silently asked herself. My *closest friend, the only one who could remember me when I was young, is gone.*

Realizing that her ideas reflected only selfishness, not a sense of grief for what Rebecca might have lost in this world, the Quaker shifted uncomfortably in her plush seat. Then, in just an instant, she began hoping that the corpse the deputy had discovered would not, in fact, prove to be Rebecca. Soon, however, Elizabeth rebuked herself for the idea. If she hoped that the body was not Rebecca, wasn't that the same as hoping it was someone else? Surely that was wrong.

Why am I thinking like this? she asked herself. My *mind shouldn't jump about as if I'm in a nightmare! I'm too old for this childishness.*

But Elizabeth discovered that her thoughts were impossible to control. As the Crown Victoria raced to their destination, her mind leaped unbidden to the years she had shared a room with Rebecca in college, then jumped to the previous day when the pair had driven across the Cascade Mountains. Minute after minute, her thoughts raced forward, finally leading her to question her own rationality.

In an effort to get her wits together, Elizabeth decided she must speak. Forcing her emotions to submit to her will was nothing new to her. Instinctively, she chose to lead her confused mind into abstractions rather than discuss the concrete realities of this dreadful evening. No matter what younger Friends in Cambridge often said about the glories of emotional life, Elizabeth believed that raw feeling had its time and place, but should never be given free reign in public.

"What can you tell me, Mr. Tomlinson," Elizabeth forced herself to ask, "about the way Hanford's internal affairs have been managed?"

If the sheriff was surprised by Elizabeth's question, he didn't show it. Perhaps he assumed it reflected the period of denial some people clung to so firmly under traumatic circumstances.

"I've lived in Benton County all my life, excluding the few years when I was in the service or at college," replied the lawman. His deep voice filled the large car. As he spoke, he shifted his impressive weight, and his hand-tooled leather holster squeaked softly.

The old Quaker unconsciously leaned away from the gun next to her on the bench seat.

"My opinion is only the view of one man," the sheriff continued as he banked the large sedan into a curve, "but from what I've seen in my professional lifetime, I'd say the Hanford project, in all its different branches, is a lot like the Pentagon. Some parts of it make sense and are run in a responsible and rational way. But, now and then, a department runs amok. There certainly have been a series of problems at Hanford, including disinformation, as they say, that was repeatedly given to the public."

He glanced at the easterner in his passenger seat. "I think all of that is in the past. I mean, I don't think radiation is leaving the site today, at least not that anyone within Hanford has been able to measure. But sometimes, I admit, I do wonder. The feds' history around here has been full of surprises for us local residents."

"I mean no offense," said Elizabeth quietly, "but for this Quaker, the pattern is clear. The Hanford site was built in secrecy, for the sole purpose of making weapons to kill people, isn't that right?"

"That's one way to look at it," said the sheriff easily. "The plutonium they made here went into the Nagasaki bomb."

"Indeed." Elizabeth nodded quickly. "The weapon that Hanford was designed to produce was one of mass destruction. All nuclear weapons have been condemned by even the mainline churches of this country because they are designed to kill hundreds of thousands of civilians."

"What's the point here?" interjected the sheriff, possibly with a trace of annoyance.

"Forgive me, I didn't mean to preach." Elizabeth was relieved to find her mind now wholly under her control. Taking a slow, deep breath, she continued to occupy herself with this abstract conversation. "Mr. Tomlinson, you used the word 'surprises' to describe Hanford's history. Perhaps the continuing revelations about Hanford should be no surprise. The mission this place was given was morally wrong to begin with. Combine that with the secrecy of developing weapons of any sort, and the result is deception, injury to workers, and even the death of civilians downwind. It's the original, clear decision to do evil, you see, that blossoms through time into all these other horrible effects."

"My father was in the Pacific Theater in World War Two," said the sheriff crisply. "He was part of the force being organized for the invasion of Japan near the end of the war. That invasion was not necessary, of course, once the A-bombs had been dropped and Japan surrendered. He always believed the Bomb saved his life, and the lives of something like a million American soldiers and Japanese as well! There's nothing evil in that, Mrs. Elliot."

Elizabeth was silent, wondering how she might voice her view that dropping the Bomb and invading Japan were both, utterly and necessarily, outside the spirit of the Gospels by which she was commanded to live. It wasn't only the words of Jesus—who again and again told his followers to return good for evil, to love their enemies, and to go the extra mile for those who exploited them—but also the very example of his life. All the good he accomplished was underwritten by nonviolence. His was a ministry of healing the sick and giving hope to the poor, not fighting the occupying Roman troops. In just the same way, at least from Elizabeth's perspective, many saints had lived: joyfully and faithfully, in keeping with the good news that evil did not have to be matched with evil, that violence did not have to be answered with more violence.

But from a secular perspective, Elizabeth knew, her deepest commitments made no sense. The man beside her—a good and honorable man, she was happy to assume—would not care to hear about the pattern of life made clear to a Quaker by the Gospel. So Elizabeth decided to steer the conversation to a place where the sheriff and she might have more in common.

"Well," she said in her gentlest voice, "we may disagree about the events in the 1940s. But what can you tell me about some of the recent things that Meghan—and I suppose others like her—allude to? Have the Hanford authorities retaliated against professionals who reported leaks of radioactive material?"

"The record is pretty clear," answered the sheriff. "There have been some cases of whistle-blowers being followed by Hanford's security officers, and workers put under electronic surveillance. Some people have been intimidated, no question. In that sense, there is a definite record of arrogance on the part of Hanford management."

"And disregard for the law?"

"Well, sometimes. The rights we each enjoy under the Constitution clearly aren't always uppermost on the minds of Hanford administrators. They have to get a job, a tough job, done."

He glanced toward his passenger and added in a clear, low voice, "But all of that is the exception, Mrs. Elliot, not the rule. And I don't think even the most strident whistle-blowers are having their constitutional rights violated these days. Not in my county."

Sheriff Tomlinson slowed the big car and turned it into the darkened gravel drive of the Nichols house. There were no streetlights in the country, of course, and Rebecca's family had clearly never invested in any safety lighting for their property. Quite abruptly, the darkness of the evening struck Elizabeth as intense. Knowing how vast the countryside around them was, the night that cut them off from the larger world seemed even more chilling.

"Try to remember, Mrs. Elliot," the sheriff was saying when she returned her attention to him, "most people who have worked at Hanford count it as just another part of their lives. It's a job, no more. Good pay and benefits, and routine work from day to day. Drama is the exception at Hanford, rather than the rule."

"I'm sure that's true," answered Elizabeth softly. "But apparently the gentlemen who administer the nuclear plants here have a history of exceptional behavior."

The Crown Vic ground to a halt in the gravel, pulling up behind the deputy's car and what proved to be the county coroner's van. Elizabeth struggled to get out of the sheriff's car, but the weight of the large door was an even match for the arthritic pain in her right shoulder. In a moment, the boyish deputy was holding the door open and offering her a hand. As she got to her feet, Meghan's pickup pulled in behind them. Panda leaped from the bed of the truck, pointed his nose into the dark, and howled into the night.

Abruptly, the events around her threatened to confuse

Elizabeth's mind once again, leaving her later with a blur of distinct but disjointed memories. She identified the body of Rebecca Nichols, illuminated by a spotlight mounted on the deputy's car. She did not recall many things about the identification, but she retained the searing image of Rebecca lying on her stomach, her head turned to one side. Even in the semidarkness, a still darker patch of blood from the back of Rebecca's head was clear. It stained a large expanse of the dirt and gravel on which she lay. Elizabeth could not help but think that her friend had been shot from behind, probably as she was walking toward the side door of her family's house.

Although it was far from the first time the old Quaker had seen death, and seen it up close, it was as wrenching as ever. For a moment, she knew, she had been awash in anger, a rage more focused on God than on any individual human. The anger came over her in repeated waves. It wasn't the first time in her long life she had felt rage toward the Spirit with which she shared her every waking moment. Close relationships, she knew, had always to weather negative, as well as positive, emotions. Finally, her sense of anger diminished just enough to allow her mind to function, however slowly.

Elizabeth allowed herself to be gently but firmly steered by the sheriff back to his car, where Meghan was standing.

"Thank you, Mrs. Elliot. We'll have to take you and Dr. Zillann back to my office for a formal statement about your actions today. I'm sorry it's so far to travel, but that's the way it must be. This is now a homicide investigation, too important to cut any corners. But you can go inside with the deputy and quickly gather up a few things to tide you over tonight and tomorrow. No one can stay here, of course, until our initial investigation is completed."

"You'll stay with me," said Meghan, reaching out to the dazed Elizabeth. "And we'll get the scum from Hanford who did this, Mrs. Elliot. Intimidating workers, bugging telephones, following people around town—they've gotten away with a lot. But those goddam federal boys are not going to get away with murder!"

"God willing," said Elizabeth automatically. Then, just as she finished speaking, true grief hit her like a gust of grit-filled wind.

7

It requires moral courage to grieve; it requires religious courage to rejoice.

Kierkegaard

Although Meghan was kind, the night was terribly painful for Elizabeth. The two women gave statements at the sheriff's office about their movements during the day. Elizabeth explained again when she had last seen Rebecca Nichols alive. She carefully described the two Hanford security men who had taken Rebecca away in their jeep, the one called Al Cartwright and his supervisor. The deputy laboriously wrote down everything that was said. The manuscript then had to be typed, read for accuracy and corrected, and finally signed.

"We'll be in touch," said the sheriff at the end of the ordeal as he led the young woman and the old one to the office door. "You'll both be at Dr. Zillann's home, is that right?"

"Yes," answered Meghan, and Elizabeth nodded.

"I have to ask you to not leave the area, Mrs. Elliot," said the sheriff. "But for now, I myself hope you'll try to get some rest. You need it."

The drive to Meghan's home was long and dark. Because of the wrenching news of her old friend's death, and because she had missed lunch and supper, Elizabeth was nearing collapse when she reached Meghan's spartan trailer home. The old Quaker's mind was racing as she struggled to get out of the pickup. But once on firm ground, she discovered that her body, too, was only barely under control. She realized dimly that she was sweating, and wondered if she was headed for some sort of nervous breakdown.

"You've got quite a case of the shakes," said Meghan calmly. "I know just what you need." She led the older woman into her narrow trailer and sat her down on a chair immediately inside the door. "Chill out right here," said the young doctor briskly, "and I'll fix you up."

Meghan was clearly not a cook, but she did her best by heating up a can of soup and making peanut butter sandwiches. When the warm soup and the abundant calories in the sandwich finally hit Elizabeth's bloodstream, she felt the blessed relief of calm.

"That proves it," said Meghan with clinical detachment. "Your blood sugar was a tad low." She smiled at Elizabeth but clearly did not expect a reply. "Since you're on the mend, I'll take care of our four-legged friend."

Meghan filled Panda's bowl with dry kibbles, added a slosh of milk, and set it down for the patiently waiting dog. She disappeared from Elizabeth's view for a moment, then came back to the kitchen, where she refilled Elizabeth's water glass and handed it to her with a small white pill.

"Now take this."

Elizabeth shook her head slightly and made no other move. She was feeling so much better than when she had arrived, she was content to sit and simply enjoy the continuing transition to a more normal state.

"It's only a mild tranquilizer," Meghan insisted, again offering the pill in the palm of her hand. "Your body needs it. Trust me. I'm a doctor!" she concluded with a smile.

Recognizing that an MD who could laugh at her own authority was more mature than most in the medical profession, and that the young woman had already rescued her from the wave of disorientation in which she had arrived at the trailer, Elizabeth took the pill.

Meghan quickly showed the Quaker around the small trailer and, putting fresh linen on her bed, insisted that Elizabeth have it. The last thing the older woman was aware of was the sound of Meghan's vibrant voice as she spoke softly in the kitchen to Panda. The tired, aching visitor gradually relinquished her responsibilities and concerns and fell asleep under the influence of the tranquilizer.

Elizabeth awoke just before the sun rose. She looked around in the near-darkness. It took a moment to remember where she was, and why she had arrived in a small and dusty trailer so very far from her native Cambridge.

The old Quaker was a bit groggy, a feeling she attributed to Meghan's medication, but she had to admit she had had a sound night's sleep. Elizabeth dressed quietly from her suitcase, which was open next to her bed, then slipped out into the trailer's main room. In the rays of the rising sun, she saw the outline of Meghan's form on the sofa. The young woman's regular breathing was undisturbed as Panda rose from the foot of the couch and walked the few steps necessary to greet Elizabeth. The collie returned to his post as Elizabeth went into the tiny kitchen and put a kettle of water on the stove to heat.

A few minutes later, after sipping a cup of tea and while watching the sun rise through the kitchen window, Elizabeth was able to truly pray for the first time since she had come to Washington State. She poured out her grief at the loss of her friend. From the silence around her, she called up her fear about the men she had seen within Hanford. Effortlessly turning toward the presence of the Spirit evident in the light outside, she expressed her anguish about all that nuclear weapons continued to mean to this land and its residents.

After many wrenching minutes of silent work, her heart was cleansed of her most turbulent emotions, and she was able to gradually sink into contemplative, wordless prayer. For some time, she simply drank in the rays of the rising sun and whatever else the Creator wished to send her. She neither sought strength nor looked for the presence of logos (sometimes translated as "the Word"), but simply accepted what was.

Briefly, the words of Mary at the annunciation slipped unexpectedly through her calmed mind:

"Let it be to me according to Thy word."

In a moment, all words were gone and Elizabeth was enveloped in a warmth that she had experienced many times before in her life as a Quaker. Filled to overflowing with the love embodied by this simple mystical experience, she blessed all that she knew of this strange desert land. She internally embraced, one by one, each of the people she had met in Washington. She had no difficulty holding the various Hanford guards in her heart with just as much charity as she felt for Meghan. Gradually, the experience dissipated, as it must, and as Elizabeth gently returned to a more normal state of consciousness Panda came to where she was sitting and put his head in her lap.

Elizabeth lovingly stroked the dog's large shoulders while his mistress groaned, rolled over, and then sat up.

"Ugh!" said Meghan, rubbing the back of her neck and squinting toward the sunlight.

Panda trotted over to the young woman and wagged his tail encouragingly.

"Yes, yes," said Meghan in a high-pitched singsong to the eager dog. "I'm getting up."

Then, glancing toward the kitchen table, Meghan added in tones more appropriate for an adult, "Good morning, Elizabeth. How are you now?"

"Enormously better," said Elizabeth, attributing her sound state of mind and body to prayer.

"Great!" responded Meghan, attributing Elizabeth's improvement from the night before to the tranquilizer and the sleep it had induced.

The two women breakfasted. Meghan, it happened, had the day off from clinic work. But what, they discussed, could the two of them do? Just waiting for a possible call from the sheriff's office had little appeal to either of them.

"I'd like to visit Rebecca's cousin and his wife. I'm not sure they've even heard the news."

"One of the deputies will have informed them by now, I'm sure," answered the doctor. "But we can stop by their place and give them condolences. I mean, they're Reba's next of kin, right? Come to think of it, I suppose they'll inherit her property."

"No," said Elizabeth simply. "Rebecca's will was drawn up

years ago. Everything goes to her church in Seattle and to some of her favorite charities."

"You religious people are a mystery to me," responded Meghan lightly. "Leaving all you have to churches. It seems so impersonal. My parents, my brothers, and I wouldn't consider such a thing. Do you suppose that blood is actually thicker when you don't really believe in God?"

Elizabeth considered the young woman's remarks seriously. "I suppose," she said slowly, "we leave more to charities and church organizations because we consider them to be within our families."

Meghan almost threw back her head as she laughed. "Points for your side!" In a playful tone she added, "But are Quakers always so quietly serious?"

"I'm one of the more flexible ones, actually," answered Elizabeth with a smile. "And if you'll forgive me for being rather sober," she went on, "the soil samples that Rebecca and I collected before she was taken away are still in the trunk of her Saab. I'd like to send them to the professor at the University of Washington whom Rebecca knew. I'm sure that's what she would want, and it would give me something to do, you see, in honor of her."

"Got it," Meghan said with a sharp nod. "We'll all need to help reach some sense of completion."

"Precisely," said Elizabeth softly and simply.

"We should send those samples, all right, but not just for you and me," Meghan continued after a moment. "Everyone living here should know if there's contamination on the land outside the site's perimeter fence."

"Yes." Elizabeth rubbed her eyes as she looked out the

trailer's kitchen window and added, "The professor's name is W-something Block—or was it Black?"

"We can call the U. and get that, I'm sure," responded Meghan. "He was in the Chemistry Department, I think."

In just a few minutes the two women were in the cab of the big pickup, headed toward the clinic. Panda was at his post in the bed of the truck. As they left the trailer court and pulled onto the highway, Elizabeth noted that she was getting used to the view of the road that the higher vehicle afforded. Maybe height became a habit, she thought, trying to explain the northwesterners' clear preference for driving pickups rather than cars.

The bright morning sun had climbed up from the southeastern horizon, and the sky was a pale, painfully pure blue. High overhead the thinnest ribbons of clouds stretched to the west. But it was obvious to Elizabeth that this would be another dry day.

Just as they pulled into the clinic parking lot, Meghan swore loudly. Startled, Elizabeth looked at her, then forward through the cab window. Her heart contracted when she caught sight of Rebecca's small blue car.

The Saab was parked where Elizabeth had left it, but it bore almost no other resemblance to the car she knew. The windshield and one side window were smashed, and small squares of safety glass were scattered around the car.

Meghan simply stopped the pickup in the middle of the small lot. From their high seats, the two women saw that several deep scratches ran across the trunk of the car. With difficulty, Elizabeth silently puzzled out the letters formed by the vandalist:

Seara Club Go Fuking Home

"I'm afraid our public schools don't teach spelling like they used to," said Meghan through her teeth.

In a burst of words, Elizabeth quickly explained to Meghan that she had seen one of the government's security men just across the street the previous afternoon. She pointed to where the pickup had sat. At Meghan's request, Elizabeth described the smaller, white pickup as best she could, and repeated her description of Al Cartwright.

"Well, he drives what sounds like a Dodge Dakota truck," said Meghan reflectively. "He's probably quite dim, like most of Hanford's low-level guys, but it's not hard to follow a little foreign car like Rebecca's in this county. It's not like we've got a lot of 'em around here."

Meghan turned off her engine, which died with a low snarl. The women got out and inspected the Saab more closely as Panda sniffed around the car. As they walked to the back of the vehicle, both women simultaneously saw that the trunk lock was smashed. With a curse, Meghan flipped open the trunk. It was empty.

"What sense can this make?" asked Elizabeth of the dry, seemingly pure air around them. "Anyone could take samples like that again, one way or another!"

"None of this is about sense, not common sense or good sense or even the sensibilities of the law," said Meghan evenly. "And it's not about stealing. It's all a warning. A warning to you, Elizabeth, to stay out of what Rebecca started—and to go home while you still can."

Meghan used the telephone inside to call the sheriff's office. Her clinic was outside the incorporated area of Richland, and therefore part of the county's not the city's, jurisdiction. Panda continued to nose around the damaged car, sniffing both at it and the ground nearby. Elizabeth, who had a cat in Cambridge to whom she was used to speaking, found herself addressing the black-and-white collie in a similar manner.

"There aren't as many unanswered questions as it first looks, Panda. It's not a question of who did this," she said, "although it's not just the one man I saw, but his superiors, too, and I don't know all of them. And there isn't any mystery about why Mr. Cartwright did this, not if Meghan and the others are right about the mentality that governs some of the people on the Hanford site." The dog continued to breathe in evidence of who had been around the battered car as Elizabeth concluded, "The only question for me is, how do I want to respond?"

Just then Meghan bounced out of the clinic doorway, her young frame a natural locus of energy. Panda trotted toward her, tail swishing from side to side.

"We're supposed to stay here," called Meghan. "Let me get my truck parked properly."

It didn't take long for a deputy sheriff to arrive. He asked Elizabeth, as the person who had parked the vehicle, several questions. Elizabeth, wondering if the wisdom of discretion or a shard of paranoia was gripping her, declined to answer, saying that she wanted to speak to the sheriff himself about the matter at his earliest convenience.

The deputy shrugged, indicating he'd relinquish this problematic woman to the authority she had named. "But you'll have to come to our office right away," he said.

"We'll beat you there," answered Meghan. The deputy nodded, and the young woman gave one short whistle, which brought Panda, at a bound, from the weeds beside the clinic building to the back of her big pickup. Elizabeth struggled only briefly to reach the high cab's seat, noting that she was finally getting more proficient at this western necessity.

The familiar drive to Prosser reawakened Elizabeth's grief at the wrenching loss of her friend. Although the Quaker was comforted by the sense of calm given her in prayer at dawn, she was soon awash in internal grief for Rebecca. As she well knew, adjusting to death required periods of intense suffering, and such grief might come over a person at odd intervals. Mercifully, Meghan was quiet as she drove them westward, and Elizabeth had some minutes to herself.

When they arrived at the stately old courthouse in Prosser, the sheriff met both women in his narrow office beside the coffee room. As he dropped into his oaken swivel chair, he indicated that he'd been informed of the damage done to Rebecca's car. He asked why Elizabeth had insisted on seeing him rather than answer the routine questions of the man in the field.

"I need to add to what I've told you about yesterday," answered Elizabeth.

"Indeed?" The sheriff raised an eyebrow. He had the knack of focusing not only his face but his whole frame on anyone across the desk.

Elizabeth quietly explained about the white pickup she

had seen across from the clinic when she and Meghan had left in the late afternoon. Interrupting the older woman's narrative, Meghan chimed in with a description of the graffiti they'd just seen scratched into the car's trunk.

But Tomlinson did not shift his gaze away from Elizabeth.

"And that's not all," said the younger woman, raising her voice in an attempt to get the sheriff's attention. "In case Elizabeth didn't get the message, the trunk's lock was smashed and the soil samples that she and Rebecca had taken are gone."

The sheriff addressed the older woman as if no one else in the room had spoken.

"Would it surprise you to learn," he said evenly, "that I've spoken directly to the chief of security at Hanford and he flatly denies that anyone remotely like Rebecca Nichols was detained yesterday on the site's grounds?"

Elizabeth answered the literal question asked of her in even tones. "I'm not sure if I should be surprised or not." She paused, looking steadily at the sheriff, then continued. "Let's assume it's not just a question of an error or some miscommunication within that organization. Then I'd say that false statements from a senior-level person are a clear comment about how Hanford is being run.

"But as I said to you last night, Mr. Tomlinson, it's not surprising to me if the evil inherent in Hanford's mission affects everything about it, even the way it relates to the local citizens. An institution that was begun in secrecy, and in bad faith, too, is not going to improve with age."

The sheriff still studied her.

"Does it surprise you, Mr. Tomlinson," the Quaker pressed,

absolutely calm under his gaze, "that Hanford denies an inconvenient, even damning truth?"

"We've got to call the ACLU in Seattle," said Meghan, addressing herself to the space in between the two other people in the room. "If the government's going to deny that it took Rebecca into custody, that can only mean there were orders to get rid of her—" She broke off, momentarily confused. "Or some low-level security goon could have been carried away, I suppose. But still, it's clear now that the highest levels of the site's administration are involved in a cover-up. Another cover-up, just like they've been doing for decades."

The sheriff smiled slightly and finally turned toward Meghan.

"The ACLU can't protect you or other local activists from murderous conspiracies and cover-ups, Dr. Zillann. If your idea is right, I should take you and Mrs. Elliot into protective custody. But that might lead, logically speaking and from your perspective, to taking everyone in the county into protective custody." A flicker of amusement passed over his face. "Then the ACLU would take us to court for overcrowding in the jail."

He looked back at Elizabeth.

"From the hard evidence I have, Mrs. Elliot, you—and maybe Dr. Zillann here—are pretty good suspects for murder. You report a friend missing, but while you say she was gone you had access to her house and you clearly felt free to make use of her car. You offer a rather unusual story that can't be confirmed—and which the highest levels at Hanford deny. And, of course, there's no physical evidence of what you claim Miss Nichols was doing on the day she disappeared. You have no soil samples—"

"Excuse me," interrupted Elizabeth. "I beg your pardon, but that reminds me to ask: did your deputies find a hand tool near Rebecca's body last night?" She described the circular spade her friend had used to take samples. Elizabeth had last seen the implement in Rebecca's hand when she was taken off in the jeep.

"I saw that tool two nights ago when I popped in at the Nicholses' place," said Meghan. "I would recognize it again."

The Sheriff responded simply: "There was nothing like that near Miss Nichols' body, and nothing like it within the house. I went through the place along with my deputies, and I would have seen it. But, of course, the absence of a hypothetical hand tool doesn't help your story."

"What I've told you is not a story," responded Elizabeth. "It's the truth."

"In a sense, I don't doubt that," answered the sheriff with a smile. "But there are facts to be considered as well as statements. My office has to follow procedures based on physical evidence. You can't prove any of what you've said."

"We shouldn't have to prove everything!" Meghan interjected. "Isn't it a plain fact that Reba was shot? Shot in the head after she'd been forcibly separated from Mrs. Elliot and the rest of us? Aren't you supposed to enforce the law—even if it's the bastards working for the feds who are breaking it?"

Sheriff Tomlinson abruptly stood up behind his desk. His leather holster and gun belt squeaked softly as he reached for his flat-brimmed hat.

"Don't fly off the handle, Dr. Zillann. You don't help yourself, nor anyone else caught up in this matter." In a warmer tone he added, "Good day to you, Mrs. Elliot. You and your friend are free to go."

8

Somehow Quakers . . . need more than ever the gift of beauty and the ability to translate it into poetry. As is everyone, we are faced with horrors of all kinds—nuclear terrors, destruction of life, and moral collapse. 'Where there is no vision, the people perish.' So far, we still have the vision and we have not perished.

Mary Hoxie Jones
Twentieth-Century American Friend

Steel-gray clouds hung low overhead when the two women left the sheriff's office. All around them, the cold desert strained in the grips of the strong wind that raced across it. Every gust of the turbulent atmosphere was laced with fine, dry dust. Elizabeth sneezed violently.

"It might rain," observed Meghan, apparently oblivious to the grit in the air and impressed only by the clouds. As she gave Elizabeth a hand into the pickup, she irreverently added, "Lord knows we need it."

Meghan walked around the vehicle, speaking a few words of nonsense briskly but cheerfully to Panda, who was sitting patiently in the truck bed.

"How can I prattle on about the weather and babble to Panda?" Meghan asked as she slid her thin hips behind the wheel. "It's indecent of me, isn't it, given all that's happened?"

"On the contrary," answered Elizabeth steadily. "Sometimes we have to talk about the normal things, and go on with life, even as we grieve for what's lost. That's just part of responding to death."

"I feel much more comfortable at the hospital," said Meghan quickly. "When I'm the doctor, in charge of a case, there's always something for me to do, even if only writing up the patient's chart." She swung shut her door. "Being a bystander, if you will, is a lot harder. Out here in the real world, I can't give brisk orders to nurses and orderlies."

"Yes," agreed Elizabeth. "Some things are quite a bit easier when we have clear roles and responsibilities."

"I want to do something!" added Meghan, and, perhaps to illustrate her words, she started the ignition.

"You've been doing a lot for me," responded the older woman over the noise of the V-8. "And the next task I've set myself is visiting Rebecca's relatives to extend my condolences. Would you be so kind as to come with me?"

Meghan readily agreed and drove eastward out of Prosser, toward Richland. In twenty minutes, they pulled up at Lincoln and Pamela's trailer at the edge of Benton City. An old pickup, which Elizabeth recognized as belonging to young Tom, sat next to Lincoln's vehicle. Tom's truck, Elizabeth noted with pleasure, had no gun in the cab. Like Meghan's pickup, it lacked even a gun rack. Lincoln's truck, of course, stood square and proud, displaying both its gun rack and a long, thin rifle.

At the dining room table, over a cup of coffee—Elizabeth would have much preferred tea, but it wasn't offered—the two visitors sat with the three family members and discussed the horror of what had happened to Rebecca.

As they quietly talked, Elizabeth noted what seemed to

be intense pain in Lincoln's weathered face. The aluminum frame of the trailer creaked in the wind, almost as if it were sighing. The conversation was slow, but necessary and helpful.

"It's strange for me to think I was right here, that whole day," said Pamela. "It's just a couple of miles to the Nichols place. I feel I let Reba down somehow, not helping her when she was so close by."

"That's silly, Ma," said young Tom. "You didn't even know she was at home."

"What with hunting season," said Pamela to Elizabeth, "even if I'd heard the shot I'm afraid I wouldn't have thought anything of it."

"With the ridge between us and Reba's place," said Lincoln, "you wouldn't have heard that shot any more than I would have over in Richland."

"Linc was looking at trucks all afternoon," said Pamela by way of explanation. "Although why he isn't happy with the one he's got is beyond me!"

"You learn what's new by looking at this year's model," said Lincoln crossly. It was, apparently, an old issue between them.

Elizabeth turned to the youngest person at the table and said, "I imagine you were at work, Tom."

Tom nodded. "Yup. And I stayed late working on a rig. Got time and a half. Didn't know anything had happened till I got back here around ten."

"You shouldn't take so much overtime," said Lincoln. "You've got a good wage."

"I'm saving up for a down payment for my own place.

When you two move next spring, I've got to buy something around here."

The conversation wandered on, and Pamela said that as soon as the police permitted it, she would close up Rebecca's house more securely. The water, she declared, should be drained out of the house's pipes before the cold weather set in. She also mentioned some of the choices the family was considering for funeral arrangements. Earlier in the morning, she explained, she had made Lincoln call Rebecca's church in Seattle and tell the minister what had happened.

"In some ways I didn't know Rebecca too well," continued Pamela, "what with her living all the way over there on the wet side. But her mother was our nearest neighbor since Linc and me moved here." She looked at Elizabeth and added quietly but steadily, "Reba's mom was a rock when I went through two miscarriages, and then later with our daughter's death. I don't know if I'd have made it without her."

The two men at the table looked down at their coffee cups.

"But then," continued Pamela, ignoring the reaction of her menfolk, "I got a lot closer to Reba when her mom was ill. It was a slow death. Since we were so near, I did a lot to help out towards the end. Rebecca came over from Seattle to visit many times, of course, and we were on the phone to each other when she wasn't here. Her mom was a real trooper, I'll say, always more concerned about how Reba and me were doing than about what the doctors had to say."

"I've got to get some pellets for the stove," said Lincoln, rising to his feet abruptly. "You want to come into town with me, Tom?"

The young man nodded his head but then, with a glance in Meghan's direction, announced he should stay and rewire the light switch in the front hall.

"It wasn't put in right to start with," he explained to the two visitors. "These manufactured homes, you'd think, would be as perfect as peach pie. But they wired up the front porch light so that when you turn it off, the inside light goes off, too. I've promised Mom for the past few weeks that I'd redo it, and I guess this is a good time, what with my taking the day off."

Without further conversation, Lincoln left the trailer by the side door. His truck's engine, which Elizabeth remembered Rebecca describing as an extra-large one, announced his departure with a deep, bass growl. Although Tom set to work, he stayed on the periphery of the gathering of women. Trailers of any sort, even double-wides, are never actually voluminous, and a person standing near the front door of any manufactured home can hear everything said at a dining room table just a few feet away.

The women continued to talk. Unconsciously, Elizabeth and Pam hitched their chairs closer to the table. The older visitor felt a strong and uncritical sense of acceptance from the tough, wiry woman across from her. The warmth between them blossomed in a woman-to-woman moment. Even though they had not known one another except through Rebecca, Pamela and Elizabeth talked as if they had been friends for years. Meghan, suffering in present company from the social limitations of both her youth and her exalted professional status as a medical doctor, quietly and respectfully listened to the older women's conversation.

Pamela coughed toward the end of a particularly long and warm description of Rebe's mother. Then her voice twisted with emotion as she changed topics.

"Sudden death is hard enough," she said, turning slightly to include the younger woman at the table. "I'm sure you've seen your share of it, Doctor."

"Call me Meghan, please."

Pamela smiled, but her lips were quivering. "What I can't imagine is that someone *chose* to kill Reba. Just decided to shoot her down in cold blood! Who could think of doing something like that, let alone actually carrying it through?"

"I can sure guess who it was!" responded the young woman. "And he must be a son of a bitch, all right." Looking out the window at the darkening clouds, Meghan was unaware that her hostess cringed.

Elizabeth explained to Pamela about the two men she had seen within Hanford's B Plant fence, and the one named Al Cartwright who had been outside Meghan's medical clinic. When she added a description of the damage done to Rebecca's Saab, Tom stepped over to the table, a grimace on his face.

"That's such an expensive car!" he exclaimed. "Jesus, what a waste!"

"Don't talk like that in this house!" his mother rebuked. Language she might tolerate from a guest she did not have to accept from a son.

Tom shrugged toward Meghan, as if to say there was nothing a normal person could do around a Baptist mother, and stepped back to the light switch by the front door.

Elizabeth, however, turned her head and spoke more

loudly than usual in a clear effort to include the young man. She explained the denials that the Hanford men at the gate had made, and repeated the sheriff's story about high-level denials by the chief of security.

"That would have to be Parker," mused Tom, turning from his work. "Malcolm, I think his first name is, or Maynard. Something like that. He's the top guy in security at the site."

"Could the men at the site be mixed up in Reba's death?" exclaimed Pamela. "Lord!" she said reverently. "Dear Lord, help us!" She gathered her wits enough to add, "I guess I'd just assumed the killer must have been some passing riffraff from Seattle—or more likely California."

"What do you think, Tom?" asked Meghan almost eagerly. "Could the low-level guys in site security have gotten out of hand? You know, overstepped their authority by a stride or two?"

"I dunno," answered the young man slowly. "In the motor pool, we don't cross paths with the security guys. Hanford is a big place, you know." Then he shook his head as if to clear it. "But that can't be what happened," he said firmly. "It just can't. The place isn't that crazy."

"But then why would the head honcho, this Parker guy, absolutely deny they took Reba into custody?" Meghan pressed.

"You've got me there," responded Tom. He appeared glad enough to look directly at the young woman questioning him, but Elizabeth was sure he would have preferred to discuss anything else with her.

But evidently Tom felt the need to defend his employer, for he doggedly continued. "Think of it this way. If the two guys did it, the ones Mrs. Elliot saw, they'd be way out of line, acting entirely on their own. And then they might have covered their tracks pretty good. Parker really wouldn't know, you see, and so he's telling the truth to the sheriff."

Elizabeth broke into the conversation. "No matter what, as long as Mr. Parker firmly denies all involvement with what happened to Rebecca yesterday, the sheriff feels he must accept his statement. It's just my word against Hanford's at this point. So now the question becomes: how can we prove that Rebecca was taken into custody and driven deep into the Hanford property?"

"Exactly," Meghan cut in energetically. "You see, Tom, we need physical evidence to give the sheriff what he needs to act. Now here's the thing: when Reba was taken in by those guys, she had a special sampling spade she'd been using." She gave her listener a tentative smile.

"And plastic bags," interrupted Elizabeth. "I think one had soil in it, and the others were empty. They were a pretty heavy plastic, with Ziploc tops."

Meghan continued the train of thought. "Reba didn't have any of that when she got home. At least, there was nothing like that with the body." She had the young man riveted on her as she went on. "Where would the security guys have taken her on the site, Tom? What building, I mean?"

"There's only one building that has the real security offices, as far as I know. It's near downtown Richland, although not so close as Central Stores and the motor pool. Do you know where the Three Hundred Area is? Just north of Richland, on the road to the Wye Barricade?"

"It's hard for me to understand what is where within Hanford. But the Three Hundred Area is an awfully familiar set of syllables," said Meghan quickly, a hint of a frown on her pleasant features. "I think my friend Nancy Davis works there. Do you know her? She's an RN and takes blood samples for monitoring exposure levels in the workers."

"I don't know her," said Tom, "but I've been to that office, of course. Once a month, we all have to go there. The medicos are in the same building with Security. That's all Three Hundred Area."

"Great!" exclaimed Meghan. "We'll get hold of Nancy right away," she said in an aside to Elizabeth.

Tom could not help but hear. He frowned deeply, as if suddenly reconsidering what he had said. Picking up his work where he'd left off, he started to check the wiring, pointedly ignoring the women at the table.

Elizabeth turned to Pamela. "We're so sorry for your loss," she said. "We'll be back if there's anything we can do, and I'll call, if I may, to find out what you decide about funeral arrangements."

"Oh, don't jump up quite yet," said Pamela. "I can put on some more coffee."

"I wouldn't dream of disturbing you further," responded Elizabeth, "and we must be on our way."

After the required thank-yous had been exchanged, the two visitors departed, passing within inches of Tom. His murmurings of good-bye were all but lost in the gust of gritty wind that greeted them as Pamela opened the front door.

Panda sprang out of the back of the pickup and greeted

them on the ground with a series of high whines. His nose was moist, almost runny, and he put his forepaws into the air briefly, a gesture of supplication.

"Yup," said Meghan to her dog, stooping to his level, "there's going to be a real storm."

She looked up at Elizabeth, explaining, "Panda's only character defect is a fear of lightning. We don't have many electrical storms here on the dry side, and I'm sure this won't be one. It's the wrong time of year, after all. But this little pup"—she fondly stroked the loose, deeply furry skin around the big dog's neck—"still has his anxieties."

"That's the way it is with fear," agreed Elizabeth.

"Would it be OK with you if Panda rode up in the cab with us?"

Elizabeth saw there was no gracious way of refusing. And, although she had never appreciated close contact with dogs, most especially shaggy ones, she could see clearly enough that Panda was deeply afraid. Elizabeth's heart was too soft not to respond.

Meghan went around the pickup, told Panda to jump in the cab ahead of her, and climbed behind the wheel. The wide bench seat made room enough for three. Meghan accelerated liberally down the gravel drive. Panda, sitting up between the two humans, looked out the windshield with what Elizabeth could only assume was intelligent interest. This Border collie, she thought, was a combination in equal parts of indefatigable absorption in everything around him and absolute devotion to his mistress. She wondered if all dogs of this breed were similarly perfect.

"While we're here," said Meghan, "and before this storm

really hits, let's buzz across the accessible part of the site towards Vernita. If you give me a few directions, we can go to the place where you last saw Reba, outside the B Plant area. I've been thinking that there could be footprints and tire tracks there that the sheriff might count as hard evidence Rebecca was taken away by the security goons. And holes in the ground, right? I mean where Reba took samples."

"Oh!" exclaimed Elizabeth. "I wish we'd thought of all that sooner. I'm afraid Rebecca was quite faithful at filling the holes she had dug, so they won't be obvious. In fact, just by themselves, I'm not sure we could see them at all. But our footprints must have been clear on some of land we were walking. Yesterday, I mean, they would have been clear—this wind may have already obliterated any marks made on this hard soil."

It was a long drive. The expansive scale of the West was beginning to grow on Elizabeth, but she still felt moments of near panic when she realized just how many miles of desert surrounded them in every direction. Finally they came to the Vernita Bridge across the Columbia River. Elizabeth showed Meghan the beginning of the small gravel road running east. The big pickup made good time on the gravel, but by the time they pulled up to the place where Elizabeth had last seen her friend, it was obvious that they wouldn't find tracks. Dust, and even sand grains, were being blown horizontally across the land by the strong wind from the west.

Elizabeth pointed out the gully where Rebecca had squirmed through the hole under the chain-link fence. Meghan alighted from the pickup, telling Panda to stay where he sat, and trotted over to the ravine. Inside the cab, sealed from the wind, Elizabeth had time to reflect that even well-trained, intelligent dogs smelled rather strongly. Panda, oblivious to his neighbor's thoughts, intently watched Meghan as she scrambled down into the gully in front of the truck. She came back in a minute, and climbed back up behind the wheel of the cab.

"Well," she announced as she rubbed her eyes, a small concession to the grit in the air, "the fence has been fixed. There's fresh metal netting that's been wired across the old gap, with a couple of hunks of rock tossed in for good measure. But even right there, I don't see any footprints. This wind has swept everything away."

Elizabeth nodded, then pointed out her dust-covered window. Through the fence, toward the top of the hill that Rebecca had climbed only the previous morning, a jeep stood silhouetted against the dark sky. It had a gun mounted on its hood. The distance was too great to be sure, but it looked as if two men were in the vehicle.

"I'll be damned, a real Rat Patrol," said Meghan. She sighed, then pointed out the truck to Panda. "Coyotes, Panda, coyotes!"

The dog whined.

"That's the only word he knows for all types of Darth Vader forces," explained Meghan.

Turning from the window, Elizabeth nodded.

With sudden exasperation, Meghan put her key into the ignition, all the while shaking her head in chagrin.

"Shit," she ejaculated. "Boy, am I slow! The problem with them seeing us is that now they know what my rig looks like."

Elizabeth swallowed her discomfort at the young woman's language.

"But," continued Meghan, protected as usual from self-criticism by her ignorance of civility, "with their connections, I suppose they could have found my registration anytime they wanted it."

"Why would those men have come back here again?" mused Elizabeth.

"Maybe they had the same idea we did. They thought they'd have to sweep the dirt clear, but the wind is doing that for them."

Just then a few raindrops splattered on the windshield.

"We'd better get back to a firmer roadbed," said Meghan, putting the truck in gear,. "in case the rain turns out to be heavy. Lord knows, we usually get only a few drops out of these dust storms. But if there's more than that, a dirt track like this can turn impassably slick pretty quick."

9

❦

We know hardly anything of God—and what we think we know is almost certainly wrong.

A Quaker Saying

Elizabeth was alarmed at what Meghan had said about being mired or disabled on slippery mud roads, and she relaxed only when they reached the paved highway at the Vernita Bridge.

"Now what?" asked Meghan.

"If I could go back to Reba's house," offered Elizabeth quietly, "I might be able to pick up the rest of my things."

"Sure," said Meghan.

She gunned the truck south across the site. They rapidly put behind them both the sinuous, dark Columbia and the even darker cliffs around it.

"Such brooding rocks," sighed Elizabeth. "I'm almost glad to get back to the open desert!"

"You don't like the lava rocks? That's a new one to me."

"They just look oppressive," Elizabeth murmured. "What could be more barren than black, rocky cliffs?"

"How about searing sunlight on the pale dirt out here?" answered Meghan. "You're here in the rainy season, Elizabeth, but remember we have more sunny days in central Washington than anywhere outside of Nevada. The basalt lava flows, or those black cliffs, as you call them, have their virtues on bright days."

Elizabeth accepted the correction.

"Sorry to lecture." Meghan glanced at her passenger. "Holding forth comes easy to me, I guess. And I sure get some practice whenever I go into Richland on the clinic's business. That place has more PhDs than there are in any other city in the nation. No kidding! It makes even an MD defensive, and we're a pretty arrogant lot."

Elizabeth smiled, and the two women continued to sweep over the pavement slicing through the desert. As they neared the site's southwestern corner, the small sign announcing the Ecological Research Park came into view. Of course, the siren and warning sign were standing there as well, like lost storks. Elizabeth almost had to pinch herself to believe this wasn't all a nightmare.

As they pulled up to the Nichols farmhouse, they saw a big, American-made car with a gold star on the door parked in front.

"Good," said Elizabeth simply. "There will be somebody to let us in so that I can pick up my things."

Meghan parked her pickup beside the deputy's car, told Panda to stay in the cab, and helped Elizabeth down to the ground. The young deputy whom Elizabeth and Meghan had first met at the sheriff's office was in the house and met them at the door. He asked their business, and left them standing in the shelter of the front porch as he called his superior. It was clear that the sheriff's office had been keeping a strict watch on the Nichols house ever since the deputy had arrived at the scene of the murder. Elizabeth, if not Meghan, was impressed that the sheriff was, indeed, putting all of his resources into solving the nightmarish crime.

Receiving permission to let Elizabeth pack and remove her things, the young deputy allowed her into the house but insisted that Meghan wait in the pickup.

Elizabeth walked sadly through the front door of the farmhouse. The place held no strong associations for her, of course, since Rebecca was tied in her mind only with college life so long ago and with correspondence from Seattle in more recent years. But still, she knew this was her best friend's family home, and the keen, physical sense of loss she had felt the night before started to reappear in her chest. The old Quaker shook off her grief as best she could, reminding herself that she had two people waiting for her.

The boyish deputy remained with Elizabeth, even standing in the doorway of the bathroom as she collected her toothbrush and toothpaste. Not used to an official escort, particularly to such a personal place, Elizabeth was ill at ease.

"This is quite a storm," she said, simply out of nervousness. "Such a strong wind!"

"Yup," responded the young deputy, putting a pinch of finely shredded tobacco into his cheek. He stepped back to let Elizabeth pass into the bedroom in which she had slept.

The house creaked as the wind buffeted its western side with a tremendous blast.

"It's blowing dirt from the Hanford property all over the

area, isn't it?" mused Elizabeth aloud as she folded up her several blouses and smoothed them into place.

"I 'spect," said the young man.

"But I suppose that's not uncommon," observed Elizabeth as she worked.

"Nope."

The elderly woman reflected that the young man had little appreciation for the art of the time-passing chat. Then, quite unexpectedly, the deputy added something on his own volition.

"It'll be a slow drive inta town. Visibil'ty must be a-droppin' every minute."

It was not necessary to even glance out the window to confirm this statement. A deeper and deeper shade of brown was covering the dome of the sky with every gust of wind, and the darkness outside had crept into the room where Elizabeth was busily packing.

"Is it raining?" asked Elizabeth as she zipped up her last suitcase, "or is the sunlight simply blocked by all the dust in the air?"

"Mostly it's th' dirt." He smiled to himself. "Grit is good for the lungs. Or so they say."

"I'm glad my friend Rebecca wasn't found on a day like this," said Elizabeth with apparent thoughtfulness. "It would have seemed even more disrespectful to the body, if you see what I mean."

"Yup," offered the deputy.

"It must have been quite a shock, coming to check on this house for us and finding my friend," Elizabeth said, letting her voice choke up, "finding her like that."

"It was th' first time I seen a homicide," allowed the deputy. "Not pretty. Specially with a slug through the head like that, and such a high-powered one."

Elizabeth genuinely shuddered, trying to close her mind from memory while opening the young man's mind to her.

"Was it a big gun, then?" she asked, trying to capture a tone that indicated she was simply musing aloud.

"A biggish hunting rifle or maybe a military one. No slug to do ballistics work on 'cause it went clean through her head, and we ain't found it anywhere. I've started to look out in the brush for any shells, but so far there's nothin' but a few that musta been out there for a lotta years."

The deputy seemed to abruptly remember his position and responsibilities. "You got all your stuff now?" he said quickly.

Elizabeth, pretending to be unaware of any change in the tone of the conversation, said, "Yes, thank you."

The deputy quickly carried Elizabeth's two bags out to Meghan's pickup. When Elizabeth got to the truck, Meghan was directing the deputy to squeeze the suitcases into the narrow space behind the bench seat.

"Ya drive careful," offered the young man as he chivalrously helped Elizabeth into her seat. The big truck rocked in the wind as Meghan turned it toward the highway and gently accelerated on the gravel. A few more drops of rain spattered against the dust-covered windshield.

"Do you think we should wait until the weather improves?" asked Elizabeth tensely. She was appalled by the midday darkness and the strength of the wind gusts. She eyed the nervous Panda next to her on the bench seat and felt for him a sympathetic distress.

"Huh?" asked Meghan, trying to process what Elizabeth had said. "No, it's nothing but a dust storm. We'll get back to my place in one piece." She laughed softly, a sound to which Panda responded with one thump of his tail on the seat. But the young woman did flick on the headlights.

"It's a good thing, this bit of dust," continued Meghan. "It'll be dark as pitch tonight. I've been thinking. Nancy Davis is a good sort, but she's got a pair of twin one-year-olds she's got to support. That's not easy, now that she's divorced."

Elizabeth had not followed her companion's thoughts, but she murmured agreement to the idea that raising a pair of one-year-olds without help would be terrifically difficult.

"She was really glad when she got that job at Hanford," continued Meghan, turning on the windshield wipers. "It was full time, which my clinic couldn't offer her just then, and it's got great benefits, like all federal work. She has good health coverage for the kids as well as herself, and even some allowance for day care. Anyway, in her situation, the job is really crucial, so I don't want to ask her to do anything she's not comfortable with. But if she can tell us what stuff is where in her building, and draw a map of the Three Hundred Area, I can take advantage of a pitch-dark night. Just slip over the fence."

Meghan braked as a semitrailer loomed out of the dust in front of them. Elizabeth breathed a little more deeply as the young woman dropped back behind the lumbering vehicle. The sparse rainfall had stopped, and Meghan turned off her windshield wipers, leaving streaks of mud across the glass.

"Once I'm in the right building," Meghan continued, "I'll

see if I can find any of Rebe's things. That would be factual, hard proof she was there. Add that to the site's official denials, and maybe the sheriff can file a murder charge. One thing for sure, with real, physical evidence we could start a wrongful death suit in civil court. Sort of like bringing O.J. to justice, using the civil courts even if the criminal courts fail."

Elizabeth had deliberately not followed the trial of O.J. Simpson, so she concentrated on the part of Meghan's remarks that she could follow.

"There's no reason to do anything illegal, and certainly risky, if we can't see the logic behind what we're assuming," said the old Quaker steadily. "Why would the security men return Reba to her family's house, then shoot her?"

"To make it look unrelated to them!" replied Meghan. "How better to lead people like the sheriff to assume it had something to with the house, or just with Rebecca Nichols, or with the hunting season. And remember, the killing may not have been planned."

The truck ahead of them turned off the highway onto a side road and slowly disappeared into the dust. Meghan accelerated, although not as much as Elizabeth had come to expect.

"Maybe," continued Meghan, "the security goons took Reba home after running her through some unpleasant interviews. That would be just like normal for them: they wanted to intimidate her, showing they could keep her detained all day, then deposit her back on her property because they knew exactly who she was and where her family's house sits. They'd say a few things as they dropped her off to frighten her more. But she wasn't the type to scare easily."

"No," agreed Elizabeth. "She never was. And, I think, old age was making her more free. Unlike a lot of older people, she really had accepted that almost all of her life was past. There's some measure of safety in that."

"Sure, I guess that's so," said Meghan easily, but clearly without understanding the alien perspective of old age. "Anyway, say the men you saw took her back to her family's house. She was angry, of course, and instead of being scared and submissive, like they wanted, she threatened to go to the newspapers. Or maybe start a petition drive in Seattle, where all those California transplants live. Or get a big-city lawyer and sue the goons in the jeep. Whatever. Somehow, she hit a nerve. One of the security boys got excited."

"And shot her?" asked Elizabeth skeptically.

"Well, Al Cartwright sounds a little disturbed, doesn't he? Following you and wrecking Reba's car like that? It's not as if Hanford's security force is full of the most noble specimens of manhood. What kind of guys do you think the feds get to do their dirty work?"

It was a perspective Elizabeth had not considered. As she thought about it, Meghan abruptly swore and slowed the truck. A beat-up Chevrolet from the 1950s appeared in the dust ahead of them.

"Look, Elizabeth," she continued, putting her frustration as a driver into her normally pleasant voice, "if Hanford's men didn't have something to do with what happened to Reba, why do they deny they ever took her into custody?"

"I admit," conceded Elizabeth, "that's an important point. We know one thing with certainty, and that's that the denials are all false. Of course, Hanford seems to have existed in a culture of lies and deceit from its very beginnings. None of which," added the pacifist determinedly, "is surprising, given the site's reason for existence. Evil naturally begets evil."

"Well, most folk wouldn't agree with all you've said," Meghan answered slowly. She glanced down at Panda, evidently discomforted by the descent into what she considered Elizabeth's theology. Both women were silent.

The two of them were, by this time, at the edge of Meghan's trailer court. The pickup turned in, shuddering in a gust of wind. Grit blasted into Elizabeth's nostrils as soon as she opened her door and stumbled to the ground. Meghan and Panda had run for the trailer, Meghan somehow carrying all of Elizabeth's luggage. The young woman opened the trailer door as Elizabeth stepped up to it. The old woman was grateful to step inside, led by Panda and followed immediately by her bags, which Meghan shoved inside.

"Whew!" exclaimed the young doctor as she slammed the door behind them all. She cleared her throat noisily. Panda was already in the kitchen, and could be heard drinking from his water bowl. Sitting down at the kitchen table, Elizabeth looked out at the low, densely brown sky. She slowly cleaned her glasses and rubbed her irritated eyes as the trailer creaked in the ferocious gusts. Panda by this time had bounced into the living room, where he lay at the foot of the sofa, curled around to lick his hind legs.

Meghan produced two microwavable portions of food for their late lunch, apologizing for the manufactured nature of the repast. But both women were hungry, the single most important variable in any meal, and they quickly dispatched the carefully portioned entrees. As soon as her stomach was mollified, grogginess began to overtake Elizabeth. The droning of the wind filled her ears, impossible to clear. Nevertheless, she forced herself to remain as alert as she could manage as Meghan telephoned her friend Nancy Davis.

"I've got to see you, Nance," said Meghan, raising her voice over the sound of the wind buffeting the trailer. "I can't explain things over the phone. When do you get off work?" After a pause Meghan concluded, "Good. I'll meet you at five at the diner downtown. I know you've got to get back to the kids, so I promise I won't keep you long. Bye-bye."

Elizabeth's head was unbelievably heavy as Meghan hung up the telephone. But inspired by a lifetime of discipline and self-control, she straightened up as the younger woman sat down beside her.

"Nancy's a good egg," said Meghan. Then, taking in her companion's state, she changed her tone. "You look done in, Elizabeth, and no wonder. Take a nap while I straighten this place up."

The old Quaker hesitated as the metal frame of the trailer protested under another gust.

"Those are doctor's orders," barked Meghan, trying to imitate the visage of an autocratic MD. But then she smiled. "I really think you could use some rest. Here, I'll carry your bags and lay them out for you."

Elizabeth could only walk stiffly and slowly behind Meghan, her every shred of energy focused on getting to the little bedroom and crawling under the covers. She knew, from her experience throughout the day, that active grief might well up within her at any moment. Perhaps selfishly, she wanted to reach the oblivion of deep sleep before a keen sense of loss overtook her once more.

10

❦

For the great majority of people the geographical community is the community of identification. For nonconformists, it often is not. The community to which the nonconformist looks for support is a community of like-minded people who may be scattered all over the earth . . . The important thing is that everyone needs the feeling of belonging to a community of like-minded people.

Elise Boulding
Twentieth-Century Norwegian-American Friend

The small trailer was quiet when Elizabeth awoke. It took a moment for her to realize that the sound of the wind was gone. She paused for the shortest of thanksgiving prayers, then stiffly stepped out of the tiny bedroom into the main part of the house trailer.

"Sleep tight?" asked Meghan when she caught sight of her visitor. Panda thumped his tail against the carpet in greeting, but stayed where he was.

Elizabeth Elliot nodded her head gratefully. "Are you sure you didn't put one of your tiny white pills in my lunch?"

"Nope," laughed Meghan. "That was your very own body that decided to sleep. You just needed it."

"I'm much better now," agreed Elizabeth. She knew that part of grieving, at least for her, could be experienced as overwhelming fatigue, but the deep slumber of her nap had been restorative. "And because my head is clear, Meghan, I'm certain about a couple of things I didn't quite have the strength to say when you were driving us home."

Elizabeth recognized that the young doctor before her was

used to making her own decisions. The old Quaker therefore adopted her most reasonable and persuasive tone as she continued.

"It would be wise to rethink your plans. I've known one other person who insisted on stepping onto the site despite the laws of trespass." She added somberly, "Don't follow her example!"

"You know that's not fair," responded Meghan, quickly standing and stepping to the kitchen counter. She poured herself a cup of coffee and waved the half-filled pot at Elizabeth, who shook her head. "Rebecca did what was right." Meghan set her feet apart in an unconsciously defiant stance. "The men working in the security detail are guilty of a terrible wrong, Elizabeth, something we both could agree is a real evil. All I want is to see justice done."

Elizabeth had sat through five decades' worth of Quaker meetings dedicated to seeking and promoting justice. She doubted the young and indignant woman before her had a reflective understanding of that to which she was appealing. But, as she well knew both as a Quaker and as a mother, each generation had to discover a great deal on its own. She could be available as a resource, and hope to influence a few small decisions, but she couldn't take responsibility for an independent young person.

Elizabeth pulled up a chair as Meghan set her feet more closely together and sipped her coffee. Panda came over to be petted, first by his mistress, and then by Elizabeth. As a flanking maneuver, the older woman decided to steer the conversation to the dog's upbringing. She asked how Panda had joined the Zillann household.

"He and two of his littermates came to my family's ranch when they were just pups," answered Meghan readily. As a dedicated dog lover, she simply assumed that Elizabeth's interest in Panda was perfectly genuine. "I was in college then, but my brothers raised the three of them. It's amazing what good sheepdogs can do on a ranch, but it's all just a combination of the basic urge to circle the herd combined with some obedience training from the start."

"What gives them the instinct to herd?" Elizabeth wondered aloud.

"It's really not herding, I guess, so much as encircling prey," explained Meghan. "When wolves stalk or hunt, they do it in teams. They work together to circle whatever it is they're hunting. Then, when the moment is right, one of them charges. If it's done well, the prey runs into the fangs, so to speak, of most of the wolf pack."

"I see. But that means the sheepdog's behavior has its basis in hunting and killing animals—something the farmer really needs to repress?"

"The rancher, not the farmer," Meghan corrected with a smile. "It's a distinction with a difference. But yes, what you said is exactly right. It's the instinct to hunt, and hunt as a group, that guides what sheepdogs do. They accept commands from us because they think we're the pack leaders. Their little minds," she said, lovingly scratching Panda's head, "are wired for accepting directions from the top dog. I suppose with wolves the sounds are yips and yaps rather than the whistle tones we humans use, but happily it's all the same to pups."

Meghan paused to refill her coffee cup, then continued in

a voice that showed she was more than glad to address her subject. "All my brothers had to do with Panda and his littermates was teach them to go forward, or to the right, or to the left, in response to certain whistles. When a sheepdog gets near the herd of sheep and runs to the right, the sheep move to the left. They respond, you see, just as if the dog were a predator like the wolf. They want to stay away from him. So where Panda goes, the sheep depart, if you see what I mean."

Elizabeth nodded, careful not to interrupt.

"If," continued Meghan, "I whistle for a dog to go forward, move to the right, and so on, I can control the movement of a hundred sheep or more, no problem. If the sheep get lethargic in warm afternoon sunlight, I can even whistle for Panda to bark, which stirs things up. He's good at the barking command!"

Here Meghan put two fingers into her mouth and let out a low but rising blast. Panda jumped up, loudly barking. Only firm commands to stop, liberally sprinkled with plenty of patting, could convince him to quiet down.

"The sheep, of course, are worried by a barking dog and move directly away from it if they can," explained Meghan. "And, of course, a good sheepdog knows basic commands like 'Come' and 'Stay'. Our friend Panda knows those ideas as words, not just whistles."

"But why isn't such an intelligent dog working on a ranch now?" asked Elizabeth respectfully.

"Well," Meghan responded after finishing her coffee, "that's the sad part. My family has lost our ranch. My parents' house is still ours, with a few acres around it, but that's all. It's just the economics of agriculture these days. Both farming and ranching can be done at a profit only when they are on a huge scale. The Northwest is a center now for what we call 'agribusiness.' Huge corporations, like Black Angus, own thousands of acres. Today they dominate this land, I'm afraid."

"I've heard reports for years about the decline of the family farm," said Elizabeth. "I guess living in New England meant I didn't think too much about ranchers." She smiled for an instant at her simplicity. "Maybe I still imagined ranchers as part of the Old West, if you know what I mean, with lots of rugged individualism and tough families carving out a place for themselves in hard terrain."

"Well," laughed Meghan, glancing out the window at the arriving night, "the Old West is gone. I'm afraid that corporate America has arrived here, almost as much as where you come from. Come to think of it, the price of land now, and property taxes, too, have become a lot like the East. The small towns are dying, but the cities, like Seattle, just get bigger and bigger.

"There's not much choice these days but for most of us to work for wages. 'Wage slaves' is what we say. My brothers and their wives all work in town now; they're just not able to work for themselves anymore. That's really hard on their pride."

The sun had gone down, and the trailer was surrounded by the night. Elizabeth quietly asked once again that Meghan not go anywhere during the evening, especially not to the Hanford property. She explained that the loss of one life did not in itself justify risking another, and that justice was best sought with patience, not precipitous action. Although Elizabeth's voice was gentle, and her thinking both clear and reflective, the young woman insisted on her plans.

"Call it the western spirit," she said with a forced cheerfulness. "You see, we do things for ourselves on a ranch. That's the way I was raised. And working in the medical field has made me even more pigheaded."

Elizabeth knew she was quite defeated. She adapted quickly. "I can't let you go out there alone," she said. "I know an old woman like me won't be any help to you, but I can at least go along and stay with your truck and with Panda." Then she added, with a bit of confusion, "Or will you leave the dog here?"

"Never!" laughed Meghan. "In the dark, you can't see him except for this one white spot around his right eye." She stroked the small white patch as the dog studied her face. "He has rather a lopsided look in the light, don't you think?" she said rhetorically, ruffling the dog's long, thick fur, "but I'm always glad he's got this bit of white when I'm out with him after dark. Without that, I'd lose track of him." She stood up, motioning for Elizabeth to stay put. "I'll be right back."

Meghan disappeared into her bedroom, and quickly returned in jet-black jeans. She put on a navy-blue ski jacket and a dark knit cap to complete her outfit.

"You're not quite as dark as Panda," observed Elizabeth as she put on her own coat. "For one thing, your whole face almost glows. But I'd have trouble seeing you at any distance, I'm sure."

The two women left the trailer. Without any instructions,

Panda leaped to his place in the bed of the pickup. Although Elizabeth was impressed with the remarkable cross-species cooperation the dog represented, she was glad he chose the back of the truck. For a city-born and -bred cat lover, sharing a cab with a collie could never be actually pleasant.

There was still light in the western sky, but they put that behind them as the truck turned east onto the highway blacktop. They sped into the darkness, toward the city of Richland. In just a few minutes, they were within the town limits. As they passed an older supermarket, Elizabeth read its large sign:

ATOMIC FOODS

"What can that mean?" asked the Quaker, quite flustered.

Meghan laughed. "During the Cold War, the word 'atomic' just meant 'good' to most of the locals around here." She downshifted. "But that sign fits pretty well with something I saw in the paper last week. Here in Richland, in the food bank, there was a mouse caught in a live trap. In keeping with our usual safety checks, the mouse was given to Hanford for testing. Both the mouse and its droppings were 'hot.' "

Elizabeth looked at Meghan to see if the young woman was joking.

"No kidding," said the doctor in response to Elizabeth's gaze. "It's the truth. Radioactive mice are just part of life's little hassles when you live with the feds next door."

Meghan pulled over and turned into the parking lot of a restaurant. Elizabeth, who knew this area was referred to as the "downtown" part of the city, was surprised that all of the buildings were one story tall. To her, it looked like a quiet town street with surprisingly ample parking.

"There's Nancy's rig," said Meghan, pointing out a white minivan in the parking lot. "All her friends tease her about it, but she swears it's useful, especially with the kids."

Elizabeth got out of the high cab by herself, beating Meghan's assistance.

"Ta da!" the older woman couldn't help exclaiming. "I did it alone!"

"You'll be driving a pickup pretty soon!" predicted Meghan. She added with a laugh, "And maybe you'll chew a little tobacco?"

The two women entered the diner and immediately saw Nancy Davis at a corner booth. She nodded as they came over. Three cups of coffee appeared from the hands of an incredibly young but efficient waitress. To Elizabeth, it seemed odd that there was no choice in the matter of what to drink, particularly when tea was such a superior refreshment, but the two locals accepted the coffee without comment.

"So what harebrained plan have you hatched?" asked Nancy of her friend as soon as the waitress departed, adding to Elizabeth, "These doctors always like to have a plan of action. It makes them feel in control."

"That's right," agreed Meghan easily. "And we like to make the lives of the nurses hell."

"You're doing a nice job of that," said Nancy. "I've been worried sick since you called. And now I expect you're going to make me late picking up my kids."

"I'll be brief," Meghan promised, and she was. She quickly sketched the events of the past two days.

Nancy was, of course, shocked and grieved to hear of Rebecca's death.

"I don't take the local paper," she explained to Elizabeth. "I've got to save money wherever I can. So I didn't know." She shook her head, then did some mental arithmetic. "It was just two evenings ago that we all met, wasn't it?"

"That's right," answered Elizabeth. "Although at the moment, it seems like a lifetime since I arrived in Washington State."

The skinny waitress came back to the table, but Meghan quickly waved her away. "Elizabeth is going to have some pretty dark memories of God's country," she mused. She glanced down at her watch and quickly added, "What we need is some help, Nance. I've got to slip into the site and get some hard evidence the security men took Rebecca there."

Nancy and Meghan talked, but Elizabeth was soon, quite involuntarily, lost in her own thoughts. She was indeed experiencing an awfully tough journey in the Pacific Northwest. The strange, cold, windswept desert and the sudden loss of her oldest friend combined to make her feel she must be living within a nightmare.

And the worst of all, she thought, *is the lack of Quakers. How can I respond, how can I even know what's right, without Friends to talk and pray with! Should I prevent Meghan from what she plans to do by calling the sheriff? But the only way for a Quaker to decide such things is in community!*

It occurred to her that hell was not a distant place, worth

considering only as a possible destination after death. The separation she felt from what had always been the centering force of her life certainly qualified as hellish.

Then Elizabeth rebuked herself. The people in Washington State had been kind to her, after all, even though she was to them an unknown visitor. Meghan had opened her house and her heart to someone she knew only as a friend of a friend.

I'm not sure I'd have done the same in her place, thought Elizabeth. *If I could be a little more openhearted, I could learn a lot from Meghan's kindness and from her courage. She's not a Quaker, and she's not even religious, but surely she is trying to do what's right. And at great risk to herself.*

"OK," Meghan was saying when Elizabeth finally returned her attention to her companions, "that covers it all."

The young doctor was fingering a sketch of buildings that Elizabeth vaguely realized Nancy must have drawn on one of the diner's paper napkins.

"You're out of here, kiddo," Meghan continued to her friend. "Get your buns in gear and pick up your darling tax deductions."

"She's got such a nice way of putting things," said Nancy to Elizabeth as she got up. "If you can help it, Mrs. Elliot, don't let Meghan get herself hurt out there, OK? She's a pretty fine doc, actually, and she'd be missed at that clinic of hers. But I do have to run!"

Nancy turned away, then spun on her heel.

"Meghan, you will remember, won't you? You've got to understand that you didn't get any information from me. I need my job."

"Sure," said Meghan easily. "Don't sweat it. Anybody on the site could have told me these same things about the Three Hundred Area. And I could have gotten the lay of the land from the air, or from a topo map." She cocked her head and added with mock solemnity, "Don't worry, I won't mention your name even if they torture me."

"Make sure they don't. But I've got to go get the twins."

And with that Nancy was gone.

"I thought we could get supper here," said Meghan in a matter-of-fact tone. She smiled weakly at Elizabeth. "But I'm too keyed up to eat. How about you?"

Elizabeth had never been less interested in food, and she said as much.

"Good," responded Meghan. "Then I'll get that sweet young thing to give us a check and we can go. It's quite dark now. I might as well do some first-degree burglary right away. If you want," she added stiffly, seemingly almost paralyzed by her own words, "I guess you could pray for me."

Elizabeth, realizing more fully what she had missed as she daydreamed, actually shuddered.

"I'll pray," she said simply. All the feelings of isolation returned as she spoke.

"Don't sweat it," said the young woman more naturally, clearly relieved that her request had been put behind them. She added in a quieter voice, "As a doctor, I've always been ready to take help wherever I can get it. The chaplain at the hospital can swear to that. Who knows what really controls the way things come out? You see some pretty amazing recoveries in hospitals, with patients responding in ways nobody in medical school would ever predict. So I just mean to say, I try to respect what you religious people do." In a brisker voice the young woman added, "Anyway, don't get distressed. I'm sure that the three of us will be back in my trailer by midnight."

"Three?" asked Elizabeth.

"Sure," said Meghan, waving at the waitress. "You, me, and Panda. He's crucial to my plan. The dog can be a diversion for the security goons, and his ears and eyes are better than mine. But come to think of it, I shouldn't say we are only three," she continued. "Us women are supposed to have a strong sense of inclusion, right? Really, there's Nance, too, so that makes four in our team." She reverted to a more serious tone. "We'll stop at her place as soon as I'm done. It's right here in town, pretty much on our way home. Otherwise she'll be worried all night long."

As they left the diner, the smell and taste of dust was still heavy in the air.

"You can feel the grit on your teeth, can't you?" asked Meghan rhetorically. "It's a nice, dense desert night. Just right for our purposes."

She climbed up the rear bumper of her truck, greeting Panda, who was waiting in the bed.

"I've got to get some things from my toolbox," explained the young woman to Elizabeth. "Stand right there and I'll hand them to you."

Elizabeth had not noticed the toolbox earlier, although it was in plain sight immediately behind the cab. She wondered if it was bolted into place. Otherwise, it seemed to her it should have bounced out long ago.

"Here's one," said Meghan, handing down a large flashlight. A heavy pair of wire cutters and several screwdrivers followed. "That's it." She scrambled out of the pickup's bed and jumped to the ground. At her invitation, Panda followed and joined them in the cab.

As Meghan pulled out of the gravel parking lot onto the paved highway, she explained her plan. Nancy had not only been able to draw the layout of the buildings in 300 Area and sketch the security offices, but she had given Meghan a good tip on how to get through a nearby section of the perimeter fence.

"Nancy said that they're doing construction next to the Three Hundred Area itself. The federal boys do a lot with earth movers on the site. It's a heavy-equipment heaven sometimes. We never know if they're unearthing some of the radioactive crap that was dumped here and there or if they're constructing more trenches to bury new stuff."

"Or perhaps doing both," responded Elizabeth. "That would be in keeping with a large bureaucracy."

"Especially one that's gone mad, like this one!"

The same oppressive blanket of darkness that Elizabeth had felt when she and Meghan had gone to the site's main gate in search of Rebecca descended on the Quaker again. Believing in evil, as she did, she knew that only grace could heal this horribly scarred land.

The pickup swung onto a series of downtown streets, then barreled up a wide, four-lane highway marked ROUTE 4.

"This is it. We're already on Hanford soil. Central Stores and all that is behind us, just to our west."

It was a superb road, by any standard, but eerily devoid of traffic. A lighted roadside sign warned its readers to listen to

AM 530 in case of emergency, and to evacuate the area if the sirens sounded. Another sign announced that firearms, ammunition, and explosives were prohibited, and that the drivers of vehicles carrying any dangerous materials would be arrested and prosecuted. Meghan accelerated past the signs without a glance in their direction. Nothing other than posted warnings impeded them from driving onto this part of the site.

After just a few miles, they took the exit marked for the 300 Area. There was no traffic at all on the side road, in either direction. Meghan braked sharply, then turned off the access road into the desert. The older woman watched as Meghan switched the truck to four-wheel traction.

Elizabeth began to appreciate what a large pickup with oversized tires could do in the absence of the civilizing influence of pavement. The truck lurched up and down over the rough earth, but the engine purred smoothly, and even the timid New Englander was not afraid the truck would roll. The headlights swept across the dirt in front of them, then swung up to the horizon, then rushed into the dark, starless sky.

Soon the dancing headlights intermittently showed that the ground was scarred by the fresh marks of what Elizabeth could only estimate must have been a small army of heavy machinery. Meghan pulled onto the ripped-up earth and stopped.

"This will never do," she said. She switched off the headlights and crawled along in the dark, following by feel alone the ruts made by the heavy machinery. "Don't worry," she said softly. "I'll know right away if I go off the path these guys have blazed for us."

"What if you drive into an open ditch?" asked Elizabeth quietly.

Meghan made no response, but she did slow the truck still further.

Slowly, as Elizabeth's eyes adjusted to the pitch darkness, she began to make out a few things. The interior of the cab was a darker darkness than the world outside. But there were no stars overhead, so there was no way to distinguish the sky from the land around her.

The beginning of Psalm 130 instantly sprang into the old Quaker's mind.

Out of the depths have I cried unto thee, O Lord.

At Meghan's request, Elizabeth switched on the large flashlight that had been resting in her lap. Doing as she was instructed, she tried to keep it pointed just above the hood of the slowly heaving truck, without jumping up to the far horizon or the sky. The flashlight illuminated more of the world than she would have guessed possible.

"It's really dark out in the country," explained Meghan. "So once your eyes get used to it, a little light goes a long way."

She stopped the truck and killed the engine. The silence of a rural autumn night enveloped the truck.

"From here," Meghan said softly, "I'll go on foot. This is well outside the perimeter fence. Right now we're not on the super-secure part of the feds' land, understand, Elizabeth? So, if you stay in my rig, I think you'll be quite safe.

"I'll go forward into the construction a little bit more, then go through the fence at the first opportunity. The Three Hundred Area should be about a mile away. It will take me a while to get there. Once I do, I'll slip into the medical office through the window of the women's room that Nancy described. Then I'll have a nice long look all through that building. As it happens, I'm a good lock picker, and I'll be able to get around. I'm sure I'll be able to find the stuff that Reba had with her when they picked her up. It's probably just left on some table or chair, forgotten by everybody when they were interrogating her."

Elizabeth could imagine some other possibilities, but she was sure the young doctor was not interested in listening, so she stayed silent.

"The important thing," continued Meghan, "is this. No matter how long I'm gone, don't panic. It will take me a while, but I'll come back."

"I hope you do, and I'll pray for it," responded Elizabeth. "But we both know I can't wait here indefinitely. So if the sun comes up and you still aren't here, may I drive to the sheriff's office and explain what's happened?"

"OK," agreed Meghan. "At dawn, you do just that. But not a moment earlier."

She opened her door and swung down to the ground.

"I promise you, I'll see you in just a few hours."

Elizabeth handed over the hand tools that had been in her lap, and the flashlight. Meghan took them and stored them in her jacket pockets.

"I'm sorry you'll be in the dark," Meghan offered. "The keys are in the ignition, though, so you could start the engine if you really needed heat or light." She added, still softly but with authority, "Come!"

Elizabeth heard Panda jump down to the ground. The closing of the truck door announced Meghan's departure.

Elizabeth immediately reflected that staying outside the controlled areas of Hanford while a friend chose to trespass on government property was far from courageous. The fact that it was becoming a habit was no comfort.

I should have gone with Reba, she thought in the darkness. *That might have prevented all of this. If there had been two old women in the back of the jeep, rather than just one, a number of things might have turned out differently. And then I would have been with her when she got back to her family's house. When she needed me.*

With a shudder she pursued the thought:

Will Meghan need me, too?

Elizabeth switched her attention back to the present. Both the past and the future were out of her hands, by her simple reckoning, so she gathered her strength to address the here and now.

As she sat in the dark cab of the pickup, Elizabeth knew, more certainly than any young, able-bodied person could, that an arthritic old woman like herself could not help anything by stumbling after Meghan in this pitch darkness. Dr. Meghan Zillann had chosen to take on the risks of intruding into a controlled area; all the Quaker could do was pray. To Elizabeth, that was not a small contribution toward her young friend's efforts.

11

The word "sacramental" has been defined as meaning "the outward and visible sign of an inward and spiritual grace," and according to Quaker belief, that "outward and visible" sign is a life lived in absolute obedience to God . . .

Elfrida Vipont Foulds
Twentieth-Century English Friend

Elizabeth Elliot prayed with all her heart.

The solid darkness of the desert filled the cab, but there was no crack through which it could seep into her mind.

The intense silence all around the truck quickly allowed the Quaker to stretch her soul. She breathed more deeply and evenly than she had since the morning, and for the first time in hours she was not bothered by the dust.

Elizabeth sank into wordless but intense prayer. After a time that she experienced as neither long nor short, she felt centered. If there had been other Quakers with her, she knew, she would have been ready for what Friends call "gathered worship," a state of intense community with one another and the Spirit. But, on her own as she was, Elizabeth was content to listen, to wait expectantly, to submit.

She listened to her heart beating. Her mind flitted through many griefs and worries, but she set them aside, the better to hear.

Again and again, she listened to the silence.

When Elizabeth opened her eyes, she knew an extended period of time had passed. But as far as she could tell, nothing around the truck had changed. Using only the sense of touch, she found the window knob and rolled down the window on her side of the cab. She looked out into the blank darkness. The dusty night air and the silence of the desert were just as she had left them.

In a few minutes, the absence of all light began to bother her. She wanted to see something concrete, however mundane. She cautiously felt to her left along the dashboard for the ignition switch. She turned the key a quarter turn and was rewarded by a strong click. By feel, she sought the headlights. She was grateful that the American-made pickup had a dashboard with the same basic design as her old Chevrolet sedan in Cambridge. Her sons both drove Japanese cars, and although Elizabeth was prepared to believe they were fine automobiles, she had never understood their dense and, to her, counterintuitive arrangement of dials and switches.

After half a minute's search, Elizabeth found the headlight knob and gently pulled it. Sharp beams of light sprang away from the front of the truck, illuminating raw and broken ground. In the far distance of what the headlights could reach, Elizabeth made out the static shape of a piece of heavy equipment. Nothing moved, but the silence was suspended for a moment by the sounds of what Elizabeth first thought must be a young wolf barking.

It's not a domestic dog, she thought to herself. *But don't wolves howl, not bark?*

After considerable thought she wondered if she was hearing the yapping of a coyote.

I suppose there are no wolves in a desert, she reassured herself. *And coyotes are no real danger to people, I don't think.*

Nevertheless, Elizabeth rolled up the window, leaving only a crack at the top for some air exchange.

Minutes passed in a welcome silence, and Elizabeth decided she should not run down the truck's battery. She found the switch to the small dome light in the cab and turned it on, then cut off the headlights.

With the cab illuminated, she could no longer see outside. Worse, she could not help but look at her clothes, which were, at least by Elizabeth's standards, in complete disarray. Nothing of the carefully ironed crispness of her blouse remained, and her navy skirt was covered with brown dust.

Elizabeth was not vain, but the sight of soiled clothes was dispiriting to her. She spent a long time brushing her skirt with her hand, but her efforts had little effect. As she worked, she realized just how stiff she was becoming. She considered getting out of the pickup, just to stretch her legs, but she knew that her shoes were not designed for the rough and uneven ground around the truck.

She was attempting mental estimates of how long a dome light could run before it began to drain a truck battery when she heard one short, distant bark.

That's no coyote, she thought instantly.

In a moment, Panda bounded up to her door and stretched his large frame up to the cab window. He barked frantically, over and over, and pawed at the window.

"I'm coming," said Elizabeth quickly. She opened the door slowly, and the dog dropped to the ground. He barked again as she tried to gauge how far it was to the uneven dirt. Judging depth had never been easy for Elizabeth, and the solid darkness around them was certainly no help. She stumbled as she hit the ground, falling forward and lying full length on the raw earth.

Panda instantly pawed her shoulder.

"Stop!" said Elizabeth, "Oh, please, stop!"

She got shakily to her feet.

"I'm doing the best I can," she said to the dog, but he was already ten feet from her, turning with a short bark to see if she was following him.

The only part of the dog Elizabeth could discern was the white patch of fur around one of his eyes. But when she reached the place where Panda had been standing, he had bounded ahead. In a few minutes they were too far from the truck's dome light for Elizabeth to see anything, white, black, or otherwise. She stood still in her tracks, wishing desperately she had on sturdier shoes.

Three more sharp barks directly in front of her sliced through the silence of the night. She looked back, reassuring herself that she could still see the softly illuminated truck against the backdrop of the black night. Then she took uncertain steps toward the dog.

Going forward into this darkness, she thought, required something not unlike faith. The process of stopping, listening, and taking a few steps forward was repeated, again and again.

Finally, when Elizabeth had stumbled more times than she could count, and could only dimly make out the truck behind her, Panda pushed his head under her hand.

The old Quaker stood on shaky legs. "I can't go farther,"

she explained aloud. She knew the dog couldn't understand, but she talked for her own reassurance. "I could never get back to the truck if I go any farther. I'm too old, Panda, and much too arthritic. I'm not like your mistress, you see . . ."

Panda grabbed the sleeve of her jacket in this teeth, clenched hard, and pulled her forward. Just before Elizabeth regained her wits enough to shout at the dog, one of her feet was obstructed by something on the ground.

The stumbling block, as it were, was soft and warm.

Panda released Elizabeth, and the old woman simply sat down in the dirt. She gingerly reached out and felt the slick nylon fabric of Meghan's ski jacket. The young woman's nearest shoulder was covered with a sticky liquid.

Meghan groaned softly.

"It's Elizabeth Elliot. I'm right here beside you."

There was no response from Meghan. Panda whined somewhere in the darkness.

"Meghan, wake up!" said Elizabeth, putting into her voice all the stern, warning tones she had used as a mother.

"Shit!" murmured Meghan. Then more syllables slurred together followed by a fragment of profanity.

"You've got to stay awake, Meghan," Elizabeth said briskly, for the first time undisturbed by the young woman's language. "Stay awake, do you hear me?"

"Yeah, I hear," answered Meghan. Her breath was now both audible and deep. "The sons of bitches! They actually shot at me as I ran away. Automatic weapon fire, can you imagine? Panda raced around and flanked them, barking to wake the dead. That confused them enough to fire in his direction for a minute, and I got out of there."

"Where are you hurt?"

"Just a graze to my shoulder. I'm OK."

"No," said Elizabeth firmly. "You're not OK. You are lying in the darkness on the cold dirt, drifting in and out of consciousness."

"Well," said Meghan, her voice much clearer, "that's a nice way of putting it. But blood loss and pain take a little something out of a person, you know?"

Somewhere in the great, dark distance Elizabeth thought she heard the sounds of a helicopter in flight.

"We've got to get you back to the truck," directed the older woman firmly. "You can just see it from here; it's that little patch of dim light in the distance. Can you stand if I help you?"

"I think so."

In the darkness, using the senses of feel and balance alone, Meghan and Elizabeth managed to get on their feet and lean against each other. Panda made his presence known with two small yips. By feel, Elizabeth took the younger woman's good arm and wrapped it around her neck.

"I have to move slowly," Elizabeth explained apologetically. "It's my joints, you see."

"Slow is good," answered Meghan simply. "Toward the light, then!"

They walked and stumbled toward the truck. Elizabeth, Meghan's careless words wheeling through her mind, prayed that they could indeed move closer and closer to the Light. Prayer and action often complemented each other in the old Quaker's life, and never had they felt more naturally linked to Elizabeth than in that desert darkness.

The *chop-chop-chop* of a helicopter was now clearly audible, but for the moment it seemed to be staying in one place, perhaps hovering over the 300 Area. Elizabeth would have liked to increase her pace, but it simply was not possible. She could only hope the helicopter stayed away from them.

The truck drew incrementally nearer, its dome light growing softly stronger. As a beacon, it was unfortunately tiny, and for a while Elizabeth wished that she had switched on the headlights when she had left the vehicle. But, she realized, the helicopter could spot a pair of headlights quite easily from the air, while a small dome light, covered on top by the cab's ceiling, was much less visible.

When the ungainly pair finally reached the truck, they found that the passenger door to the cab was still open. Both women worked at getting Meghan up into the high seat.

"You've got to drive," said Meghan to Elizabeth, who still stood beside the passenger door on the desert floor. The younger woman added confusedly, "You do know how, don't you?"

"Of course!" said Elizabeth briskly and shut Meghan's door.

While it was true that Elizabeth knew how to drive, and indeed had been doing so since before Meghan was born, it was also true that her experience was limited to sedans, generally with automatic transmissions, on the well-paved roads of New England. The old Quaker uttered a fast prayer for help as she limped stiffly around the front of the truck.

As soon as she got the door to the driver's side open, Panda sprang through it. He leaped up in a single bound to the high bench seat. Elizabeth, in contrast, took much longer for the same task, first pulling herself up to the running board, then awkwardly standing, and finally folding herself into the seat behind the wheel. By the time she arrived in her place and struggled with the heavy door enough to close it, she was in a great deal of pain.

Elizabeth had learned to drive in the late 1940s, shortly after her marriage. Her husband, Michael, had spent many evenings with her in his 1928 Ford, trying to explain the choke, the clutch, and the much more intelligible brake and gas pedals.

Meghan swore softly as Elizabeth oriented herself. The younger woman was looking down at her blood-soaked jacket.

"I'll take this off and apply pressure to the wound," she said, the analytical tones of a medical doctor ringing clear in her voice. "Just turn us around and get us back to the highway, Elizabeth. Keep her in first on this rough stuff. Then we'll go to Nancy's. She can help me stitch up my shoulder."

Elizabeth nodded, thinking furiously as she studied the dashboard.

"I can't find the choke," she announced softly. "I'm sorry, but would you point it out?"

"Lord!" exclaimed Meghan crudely. "It's automatic choke. And it's already in four-wheel. Just put in the clutch and start it up!"

Elizabeth did as she was told, remembering to depress the brake as well as the clutch only when the big truck began to roll forward. To her infinite relief, the engine started with a roar, gently torquing the cab in the ultimate expression of mechanical power. There was no way now of knowing if the sounds of the helicopter blades were growing stronger or softer, but neither woman forgot the importance of haste. Elizabeth kept the headlights off, making her feel blind, but when she thought to turn off the dome light, the situation improved slightly. Between the two women, Panda sat motionless, a presence felt more than seen.

Elizabeth gingerly put the behemoth in first gear and eased off the clutch. The truck lurched forward, but the engine kept running, and Elizabeth Elliot found herself guiding the high truck over the wildly rough ground.

She turned around, simply by bearing to the right and swinging through 180 degrees. There was no curb or sidewalk to avoid, no need to estimate how much room she needed to do the U-turn. In a flash, Elizabeth saw the advantages of off-road driving, but she was far too intensely focused on her task to enjoy her fleeting freedom as a driver. The truck all but guided itself back to the highway. In first gear, it was easy for Elizabeth to keep to the wide path of broken earth that marked the trail the heavy equipment had blazed.

"Now," announced Meghan when they were up to the lighted but empty road, "you've got to take it out of four-wheel. It can't run on dry pavement in four-wheel drive, because the wheels can't slip like they need to when you turn."

Following Meghan's instructions, Elizabeth stopped the truck, a task during which she almost killed the engine, and then wrested the stick on the floorboards into its two-wheel-drive position. Not a single vehicle passed along the access road as she struggled with her work. When she finished, she flicked on the headlights.

"Turn right onto the blacktop," said Meghan crisply.

Elizabeth did so, and with less rather than more grace, she

ran the truck through several gears, gaining some speed on the highway. Turning at the huge strip of pavement on which they had earlier arrived, she headed south toward Richland. A glow from the city's lights could already be seen.

"You can go faster, Elizabeth," said Meghan. "The chopper must still be around. And it won't be long until their Rat Patrol jeeps arrive."

Reluctantly, Elizabeth accelerated, slipping into the highest gear. As the few miles to Richland melted away, Meghan appeared to drift into semiconsciousness.

"This is the city," said Elizabeth sharply. "I need your directions."

Meghan opened her eyes as Elizabeth downshifted. She guided them through town to a small residential street. A tiny house that appeared to date back to the 1940s popped into visibility in their headlights as they turned into its driveway. Elizabeth forgot about the clutch as she braked the truck, and the engine died with a strong lurch and a sharp protest. The grating sounds of mechanical protest immediately brought a figure out of the house.

"I got the kids into bed a long time ago, and I've had nothing to do but worry. I was so glad to see your rig pulling up!" said Nancy, stepping up to the driver's-side window. "Oh!" she added in confusion. "It's not Meghan."

"No, but she's right here," answered Elizabeth. "And we certainly could use your help."

Nancy, in the display of the casual strength so common to nurses, got Meghan quickly down from the cab, across the yard, and into the house, where she laid her out on the kitchen floor, directly under a fluorescent ceiling light. She got a bowl of water and a clean cloth before bending down to the wounded doctor.

"I'm just a bit weak," Meghan explained defensively. "A little loss of blood."

"I can see that," said Nancy briskly. "And some borderline shock, I'd guess. Mrs. Elliot, just to be on the safe side, sit down on the floor and set the patient's feet on your lap. I want them elevated while I work."

Elizabeth did as she was told. Panda, unbidden, took a post in the corner, studying every move the humans made. Nancy, clearly a competent and efficient nurse, lifted away the blood-encrusted jacket near Meghan's left shoulder and studied the messy area beneath.

"I've got to see better," she announced, deftly tearing Meghan's blouse away from the wound. Her strong hands quickly enlarged the hole in Meghan's clothing, exposing the patient's bra as well as her whole left arm.

"There's no need to take me down to my birthday suit," Meghan protested.

"Quiet!" said Nancy in a tone of natural authority. She cleaned the area around the wound with generous amounts of water. As it flowed out onto the floor around Meghan, Elizabeth leaned forward and tried to mop up the excess.

Nancy peered closely at the injury itself. After a moment she announced, "It's a crease, not an interior wound."

"That's what she said to me when I found her," confirmed Elizabeth.

"The patient has bled enough to keep the wound quite clean. If this were an ER, Dr. Zillann, you'd stitch the gash. Let's get you to the hospital where they can do that."

"No," answered Meghan. "You know that whoever is on duty would be obliged to report a gunshot wound to the police. Go out to my truck, would you, Nance, and get into the toolbox behind the cab. I've got an emergency medical kit there. I keep it stocked up nicely in case I come up on road accidents."

Nancy disappeared and came back with a leather case of materials. Slowly, working together, doctor and nurse assembled what they needed. Elizabeth watched silently as they spread several instruments and a roll of what looked like pink fishing line on a clean terry towel on the floor.

"We don't have any antiseptic," said Nancy in the light tone Elizabeth had often heard in emergency rooms. "Care for me to pour whiskey on the wound?"

"Don't scare Elizabeth," said Meghan. "She looks like death warmed over as it is."

Meghan pulled herself into a sitting position against the kitchen cabinet and set to work stitching shut the wound. Elizabeth, relieved of the duty of holding feet in her lap, gratefully leaned back against the refrigerator.

Since Meghan could use only her right hand, Nancy had to assist in the repair work, holding every stitch tight as it was tied off.

"Goddamn," breathed Meghan midway through the work. "It sure does hurt."

"Nothing to be done about that," Nancy responded briskly. "Keep going, Doctor, and we'll be done soon."

A few minutes more and the wound was closed.

"So," announced Meghan weakly, "there will be no more

bleeding." She relaxed against the cabinet with evident relief. The intensity of the moment had passed.

"That's a bit premature," said Nancy. "We'll need pressure applied through the rest of the night, at least."

"You'll have to manage that with a tight bandage, Nurse," replied Meghan. Her tone was as dismissive as if they had been in an ER and Nancy was not personally known to her.

"There's no bandage wrap in your kit," observed Nancy sharply.

"Just tear up a sheet," the doctor responded wearily. "I'll owe you one."

"Which I'll never see," said Nancy, relief and fatigue leading her into the first trace of testiness.

A few minutes later, with an improvised but impressive bandage swathing her shoulder, Meghan allowed herself to be wrapped in a ski parka and propped up on a kitchen chair. Panda, who had viewed the medical proceedings from the corner of the kitchen, now came over to his mistress and put his shaggy head in her lap.

Elizabeth, whose arthritic joints had been in increasing agony while she had been sitting on the floor, found she could simply not get up. Nancy helped pull her to her feet and guided her also to a kitchen chair.

"We're a fine pair, Elizabeth," Meghan allowed sarcastically, idly patting Panda's head with her good hand. "Do you think we'll be able to feed ourselves?"

Flustered, Elizabeth apologized for her rheumatic disabilities.

"Goodness sakes!" scolded Nancy. "Don't distress yourself,

Mrs. Elliot. And don't pay attention to what Meghan thinks is humor."

"I just wish I could do more," said Elizabeth, "and more reliably."

"Saving my life counts for quite a bit," responded Meghan. "Or do you think heroics like combing the desert floor at night for a wounded stranger counts for nothing in Saint Peter's book?"

Elizabeth, unsure how to respond, started to stammer a reply, but Nancy cut in. "Blood loss is no excuse for a sharp tongue. Let's all take a deep breath. I think we need a drop of medicinal brandy."

"An excellent idea!" said Meghan with feeling. She added, "There is nothing more useful than an experienced nurse."

Nancy poured out small brandies for Meghan and herself. At Elizabeth's request, the Quaker was provided with a glass of juice. In just a few minutes, blood sugar and blood alcohol content had temporarily altered their frazzled feelings.

"This little boost won't last long," said Meghan. "I suppose we'd better get back to my trailer while we can."

Elizabeth dreaded driving the huge pickup again, and she said so.

"And I don't want to lift you back up into that high seat," agreed Nancy. "Getting you down was one thing, but up is a lot tougher." She thought for a moment, then added, "I'd give you a lift home in my car, but I can't leave the kids alone."

She looked from the disheveled doctor to the dispirited Quaker at her table and almost laughed. "There's room at this inn, you two! The sofa bed is in the living room, if you don't mind sharing."

In only a few minutes the efficient Nancy had opened the bed, covered it with sheets and blankets, and found two nightgowns for her visitors. With the help of the indefatigable nurse, Meghan was laid into bed and Elizabeth helped off with her clothes.

"I'm sorry to be such deadweight," Elizabeth apologized, "but it's so hard to undress when my shoulders are hurting so."

"I'm sure you stirred up a lot of joint pain helping Meghan to the pickup," said Nancy. "She's very lucky you were there."

"Uh-huh," grunted the young doctor. In another minute Elizabeth eased onto her side of the sagging sofa bed. Panda curled up on the floor next to Meghan, his eyes still fully open and alert to his duties as the night shepherd. Nancy quietly stepped out of the room and turned off the lights.

Although Elizabeth meant to pray, she fell into a deep sleep even before Nancy had gone upstairs.

12

We cannot know whether we love God, although there may be strong reasons for thinking so, but there can be no doubt about whether we love our neighbor or no.

Saint Theresa

Elizabeth had to struggle with all her will to awaken. As she doggedly clawed her way to consciousness, she experienced the half-waking nightmare of not knowing where she was. The room around the sofa bed on which she lay was strange; she was sure she had never seen it before in her life. The cheap construction of the house and the wide, if weedy, yard out the window made it clear she was not in Cambridge. With a final surge of will, she struggled to sit up against the combined forces of the sagging mattress and her own arthritic pains.

Children's shrill voices pierced the air from the next room. Only as Elizabeth sat on the edge of the bed and rubbed her face did she remember all that had happened on the previous, terrifying, night.

Help me! she cried, instinctively and silently.

An answer from an unexpected direction was given in Meghan's voice, reaching her from the living room doorway.

"She's awake, Nance!" Meghan called.

Walking over to the sofa bed, her arm still swathed in the previous night's makeshift bandage, Meghan added, "We thought if we let the kids make enough noise, you'd eventually have to come to."

"Actually," Nancy interjected as she came into the room, "we just couldn't keep them quiet forever. How are you feeling, Mrs. Elliot?"

"In circumstances such as these," said Elizabeth with a fleeting smile, "surely we must be on a first-name basis."

"You got it," Meghan said. "But answer the question. Our efficient nurse—and dedicated mom—has been worried about you. Me, she dismisses as being on the mend, but she's been peering at you with real concern for hours!"

"Morning," answered Elizabeth soberly, "is always the worst time for rheumatism. My arthritis pills must be in my belongings at your trailer."

"I'll drive us there as soon as we've had something to eat," responded Meghan promptly. Seeing Elizabeth's questioning look, she added, "I'm fine. I can drive my rig, no sweat."

"She's not fine," said Nancy. "But she's doing much better. If she rests, she'll bounce back. That's the advantage of youth."

"Indeed," replied Elizabeth. "One's age makes all the difference."

"I did some good work with those stitches," added Meghan. "My only real problem at the moment is trying to figure out who I can bill."

"Conundrums like that," Nancy shot back, "won't be solved until we have national health care."

"And Jesus will return before that happens!" said Meghan with a smile.

Elizabeth, who had always thought that medical care should be available to all who needed it, was too slow of speech to enter the younger women's banter.

"Thank God!" Nancy was saying without reverence. "The day they make health care a right rather than a privilege is the day they'll be able to jail us for smoking or just growing fat."

"Ain't that the truth!" responded Meghan. "Right, Elizabeth?"

"I'll just get back into my own clothes, and be ready to go," Elizabeth replied as a way of avoiding the question. Her own perspective was so different from this northwestern one that she dared not voice her views.

"Go keep an eye on the kids," said Nancy briskly to Meghan. "I'll help Elizabeth get dressed." She added in the older woman's direction, "If I may, of course."

Elizabeth was glad to accept the help. It was particularly unfortunate, she had always thought, that getting dressed—the most challenging set of stretching, wriggling, and bending movements a rheumatic patient ever attempts—had to occur first thing in the morning. But with the help of a cheerful and strong woman, well practiced in nursing, dressing was not as difficult as usual. Soon Elizabeth emerged from the living room onto the small front porch of the modest house. As she was drinking in the seemingly pure morning air, Panda stepped over to her from the grass on which he had been lying. He wagged his tail slowly as he drew near.

"Goodness," said Elizabeth with self-reproach. "I had forgotten all about you." Despite her confirmed status as a cat-person, Elizabeth reached out and stroked the shaggy head presented for her hand.

"It was a terrifying night out there on the site, wasn't it?" mused the old woman aloud.

Panda wagged his tail more vigorously, clearly unconcerned by the past but happy to hear Elizabeth's voice.

"You have a great advantage over me," said Elizabeth sincerely. "Living always in the present, not the future or the past, is something we Quakers think we should strive for. But no Friend has ever accomplished it. We don't have the kind of natural trust you do."

Panda's attention was torn away by the sound of his mistress's voice.

"Thanks again," called Meghan, stepping out onto the porch and closing the screen door. "I told Nancy not to come out and see us off," she explained, taking Elizabeth by the arm and stepping slowly toward the pickup. "Her kids are busy doing destructive kid things in the kitchen. She should stay with them. The two of us can get breakfast at my place. But I'm glad to see that you and my furry roomie are becoming friends."

"Indeed," said Elizabeth. "I think we became partners last night."

Meghan drove using her good hand. She had to go more slowly, since turning the steering wheel while shifting the gear stick was more than a bit awkward. Elizabeth was grateful for the reduced speed. As they went west on the highway out of town, she explained the way Panda had led her across the desert ground the previous night.

"For a while, I could follow him because of his one white patch of fur. Even as I stumbled around in these flimsy shoes, I could just make that white spot out, while everything else was total darkness."

"Yeah," said Meghan, "I've relied on that patch of fur myself sometimes, out by my family's ranch house."

"But when we got still farther from the truck," explained Elizabeth, "there wasn't enough light for me to see even his white spot."

Meghan braked behind a semitrailer. With a sigh, she adopted its speed.

Elizabeth related how Panda had guided her through a few feet of darkness with barks and, finally, urged her to completion of the trek by pulling at her sleeve. Meghan was pleased, although not surprised, at the dog's ingenuity and faithfulness.

"I should have let him sit with us up here in the cab!" she laughed. "Not stuck him in the bed as usual. His feelings will probably be hurt all day."

"What, may I ask, did you find?" queried Elizabeth. "And how did you come to be shot?"

Meghan sighed. "I'm sorry to disappoint you. I'm quite an amateur, it turns out, at this breaking-and-entering routine. Hanford's security is not as lax as you might think, driving across the open parts of the site the way we do."

She cleared her throat heavily.

"The Three Hundred Area has got itself one serious fence,

and the construction hadn't breached it. The fence is maybe eight feet tall, chain link, but with three strands of wire at the top. I used my flashlight, studied the thing, and decided all three strands were electrified. So I started to cut through the chain link, down at ground level. I made some progress on that, and got a hole opened. Panda got through, no problem, but as I crawled in my jacket got caught. Then, as near as I could tell, a security man came by in a jeep inside the fence."

Meghan edged out from behind the truck in front of them but fell back. Elizabeth was relieved.

"Panda gave him hell," continued Meghan, "growling like he would tear the guy's throat out. That distracted the man, and Panda kept him moving away from me. I got free and stood up. I think he saw me then, and just opened fire. You can't blame Panda for wanting to get out of there, and he knew the only hole in the fence was the one I had just made. So he came barreling back to where I was, the jeep in pursuit. The guy screamed for me to put up my hands. I ran. He emptied his gun at me. At least"—she glanced across the seat at her passenger—"that's what it seemed like. It was some sort of automatic, probably mounted on the hood of that jeep, and I tell you, I thought I didn't have a prayer."

Elizabeth, of course, thinking of the last word literally, wanted to protest. But she was wise enough to be silent.

"Somewhere in all that gunfire," continued Meghan, "I got hit. I kept running, heading in the general direction of the pickup, with Panda near me. But the pain got pretty bad, and I was probably suffering from a bit of shock after a while. The next thing I remember is you making me get up and stumble across the truck. I was sure lucky to get out of there, and even more lucky to be more or less in one piece."

"Luck may not have been the only issue," said Elizabeth firmly. She added, with equal conviction, "I shouldn't have let you go."

"How could you have stopped me?" said Meghan, suddenly almost laughing. "I was in love with the idea of breaking into the Three Hundred Area. It was like the movies!"

"Yes," said Elizabeth simply, "maybe we both were seduced by the drama of such an attempt."

"Well, that's a bit heavy to consider without breakfast," said Meghan easily, braking so as not to gain on the truck still just ahead of them.

"We may have been helped in several ways last night," mused Elizabeth soberly. "Not only with the guard's poor marksmanship. That helicopter, for example, stayed away long enough for me to get us back to the outskirts of the city."

Before Meghan could respond to any notion of divine intervention, the truck in front of them slowed still more, then began to turn off the highway to the right.

"No turn signal!" exclaimed Meghan. "Doesn't that figure! He's so slow he's a hazard on the road, and he can't even be bothered to indicate that he's turning off." Then, as she changed gears, she laughed. "He drives as bad as me!"

"As badly as I do," Elizabeth corrected unthinkingly. An instant after the phrase escaped her lips she regretted it. But as she began to apologize, Meghan swore loudly.

"That's my trailer court!" she exclaimed.

Following Meghan's eyes, Elizabeth saw their destination

ahead, on the left of the highway. The large truck they had been closely following had blocked their view. Now they could clearly see trailers. From them, a black column of smoke was rising into the broad, cloudless sky above them.

"I hope it's not anybody I know," said Meghan, accelerating modestly. In a moment they were turning into the trailer court, and Meghan swore again.

"That's awfully close to my trailer!" she wailed.

As they pulled up to Meghan's residence, it was clear that, in fact, it was the doctor's own home that was engulfed in flames.

"Jesus, Jesus!" exclaimed Meghan, slamming on the brakes and turning off the engine. She was out of the cab, running toward the inferno, before Elizabeth could think of how to respond. From the corner of her eye, the older woman saw a blur of black-and-white fur passing the truck as Panda leaped from the bed and ran protectively after Meghan.

Later, when Elizabeth had time to reflect on the fire scene, she was ashamed that her first thought had been for herself. She had been quite determined not to leave the truck. After all, she had reasoned, there was nothing she could do to put out the fire, and she was both stiff as a poker and riddled with pain.

Pointlessly rolling down her window, Elizabeth studied the orange flames and black smoke engulfing Meghan's trailer, suddenly realizing that all her medication was lost. With a quickening sense of panic, she wondered if, here in rural Washington State, she could get more of the drugs to which she was accustomed in Cambridge.

Perhaps I can call my doctor at home, she thought. Telephoning a doctor long-distance was a novel idea to her. Only after a few minutes did it occur to Elizabeth that Meghan, after all, was a medical doctor who could prescribe medicines. Knowing the young woman personally, she guessed, had confused her for a moment. *She doesn't really seem like an MD. It's not that I'm sexist, exactly, it's just that she's so terribly young.*

Quite a crowd of trailer court residents had gathered by the time Elizabeth Elliot could think of people other than herself. They were hosing down the trailers near Meghan's, trying to keep the intense fire within her structure from spreading to other people's homes. It was clear that Meghan's trailer itself was beyond hope, and the young doctor stood, one hand in her jacket pocket, her other arm in a homemade sling, simply watching the fire.

A truck from the volunteer fire department of Benton County arrived. The assorted volunteers, old and young, had come in time to dampen the remnants of the gutted trailer as it burned itself out.

Out of the crowds, a large man appeared by the side of the pickup. Elizabeth was glad to see the sheriff in his flat-brimmed hat and ceaseless uniform. He stood close enough to the truck that his gun belt was not visible, and that, perhaps, further improved Elizabeth's attitude toward the lawman.

"Good morning, Mrs. Elliot," Sheriff Tomlinson began, tipping his head, and therefore his hat brim, to her. "This is surely a rough way for Dr. Zillann to be starting the day."

"Indeed," replied Elizabeth economically.

"Were you two here when the fire began?" he asked.

"No." Elizabeth almost explained that they had spent the night elsewhere but caught herself. "No," she repeated, "we weren't."

"It just happens," mused the sheriff, looking at the smoking and crumpled remains of the trailer, "there was some sort of intrusion on the site last night. At the Three Hundred Area, I'm told. I believe that houses the headquarters for the Security office."

"I see," said Elizabeth without inflection.

"Shots were fired." The sheriff shifted his gaze to Elizabeth's face.

"By whom?" inquired Elizabeth politely.

"By the Hanford security forces, certainly, and possibly by the people intruding into the area."

"But possibly *not* by them," Elizabeth observed.

A flicker of a smile crossed the sheriff's face.

"How might I read this?" he said after a moment's silence, waving his hand at the destruction in front of them. "If you'd be so kind as to offer an interpretation," he added.

"Well," said Elizabeth slowly and seriously, "I suppose it could've been an accident. Trailer houses do spontaneously burn, and more frequently than houses, don't they?"

"My fire investigator has already said to me it looks like arson."

"Interesting." Elizabeth sighed. "One crime leads to another and another and another."

"Which is one reason not to break the law, Mrs. Elliot,"

said the sheriff. "Trespassing, breaking and entering, all of that, is a serious violation of the laws of this state. In this county, I enforce the law."

"I understand," said Elizabeth simply. "And I trust that arson is also illegal."

"I'll gladly arrest anyone I can show is an arsonist," confirmed the sheriff.

"Good. I believe that you would." Elizabeth paused, coughed slightly in response to the smoky breeze, and continued. "You asked how I might interpret this."

The sheriff nodded.

"Of course one must remember Al Cartwright's presence at the place where I parked Rebecca Nichols's car, and the subsequent vandalism and theft from it." Elizabeth frowned and rubbed her forehead, careful in what she was saying. "I have reason to think that Dr. Zillann's truck, as well as her place of work, is known to the security men on the site. It wouldn't be difficult, surely, for them to find out where she lives."

The sheriff nodded ever so slightly, but said nothing.

"If there was an intrusion on the site's property last night," Elizabeth continued, "one might be led to suppose this act of arson is a response. It's another warning, like the vandalism of the automobile and the theft of its contents."

Elizabeth looked at the darkened, twisted metal before her, all that now remained of Meghan Zillann's home.

"You seem not to think this is attempted murder," the sheriff offered quietly. "Are you just being generous?"

"I like to think not," answered Elizabeth sincerely. "I want to believe that Mr. Cartwright and his colleagues have not sunk to the level of trying to kill a harmless, old New Englander, on the one hand, and a dedicated young doctor who works for the poor. But given Hanford's history, and the murder of my own dear friend Rebecca, surely anything is possible."

Meghan appeared abruptly at the sheriff's elbow.

"I want you to get the bastards who did this!" she said, her anger white hot. "I want them nailed."

"As do I," answered the sheriff easily. Looking at Meghan's bandaged arm, he continued, "I'm sorry to see you've been hurt. How did that happen—not here at the fire?"

"No," said Meghan, "not here. It's nothing." She glanced at Elizabeth as if to confirm the older woman had offered no story about the previous night, one way or another.

Quickly, the younger woman continued. "I expect you to get Al Cartwright and his bosses brought up on charges. This fire, after all, is in the county itself, not on federal property. And there's plenty of physical evidence." Meghan waved her good hand at what had been her home as Panda materialized from the crowd and leaped up to the bed of the pickup.

"We'll start by looking for hard evidence of arson," said Tomlinson calmly. "If it exists, as I believe it well may, we'll begin the process of linking this to a specific person. If you'll excuse me," he said, nodding toward Elizabeth, "I'll go to work on it."

He turned and walked away into the crowd of onlookers.

The women drove toward Richland, Meghan venting some of her frustration on the gas pedal. Reaching the city, they spent the rest of the morning running errands connected with the fire. They went to the office of Meghan's insurance company and then stopped at a pharmacy for Elizabeth's prescriptions, including not only her arthritis medicine but the pills she used for migraines.

"Might as well get anything you could need all at one time," said Meghan briskly. "And I may borrow a tablet or two of your narcotics, for the old arm here."

Using the pharmacy's telephone, Meghan called her clinic and explained she was homeless and injured. Elizabeth noted that the young doctor allowed her office to think the injury had been incurred at the trailer fire. Although she knew most people would see no real harm in misleading coworkers on such a point, the old Quaker was uncomfortable with any deception.

Both women were close to collapse as they wrestled with the heavy door and left the pharmacy.

"Shall we go back to Nancy's house?" asked Elizabeth confusedly. It didn't seem right to impose on the busy woman, but, for the moment, she didn't know where else to go.

"No," said Meghan. "The boys who torched my trailer could find us there. We've got to keep away from them, that's for sure. I suppose we could consider Rebecca's relatives, out at Benton City. There would be somewhere we could hide my truck, but I'm not sure what our welcome would be like." She paused, ran her good hand through her unruly hair, and said, "Wait right here."

Elizabeth did as she was told, slowly and awkwardly sitting

down on a bench beside the door. Fatigue and lack of breakfast gave her no choice but to rest as best she could. Meghan disappeared into the store, but reemerged fairly quickly. She joined Elizabeth on the bench.

"I told 'em that my truck had some mechanical trouble," she explained, "and asked if I could leave it here for a couple of days until my brother comes to town. They know me, of course, so they said that was fine."

"This means we're on foot?" asked Elizabeth warily.

"Yup!" said Meghan. "It's the only way we can hope to disappear in this town." She whistled to Panda, who leaped down from the bed of the pickup and bounded over to them.

"We've got no wheels," Meghan continued more quietly, "and we don't have much to our names. Your luggage, of course, is gone up in smoke, along with my trailer. So neither of us has even a change of clothes."

"And we wore these things last night," said Elizabeth. "I'm quite filthy." She involuntarily wrinkled her nose at her own smell.

"A little desert dust, that's all," said Meghan, "and honest sweat. As I was saying, we've got nothing except your prescriptions, my credit cards, and Panda here."

"And, perhaps, God's help," offered Elizabeth sincerely. "I really do think we were aided last night."

"Well," said Meghan in a tone that might have included a note of sarcasm, "what more can we need?"

"Breakfast," replied Elizabeth matter-of-factly. "Neither of us has eaten today, and it's almost noon."

A thin man dressed in jeans and a dark shirt had been

crossing the parking lot toward the pharmacy. He stopped when Panda walked toward him. The man held out his hand, palm downward, and murmured friendly encouragement to the sheepdog.

"A fine Border collie you've got," he said toward the women. "What's his name?"

"Panda," said Meghan.

"Panda, sit!" said the man quickly. The dog, with a glance back at Meghan, sat down on the asphalt.

"Good dog!" exclaimed the man. He ruffled Panda's fur, especially at the neck. After a moment, Panda stood, then growled at him.

"Panda!" cried Meghan, still sitting. "Come here!" To the man, now headed for the pharmacy door, she added, "Sorry!"

"No problem," he responded. "I was just too friendly too fast."

When the women were alone again Meghan said, "You're right about breakfast, Elizabeth. And Panda, too, needs something to eat. I've got a plan for that and more." She stood up from the bench, then used her good arm to help Elizabeth to her feet.

"We're on George Washington Way," explained Meghan, "which parallels the Columbia. The river is just two or three blocks over." She confirmed her statement by checking the sign of a crossing street. "If we walk downriver about three blocks, we'll come to this town's biggest and finest motel. That'll be our home for a while." She added with a small smile, "I'll take the responsibility, moral and otherwise, for registering us under some random names." Then, much more seriously, "Can you walk several blocks, do you think?"

Elizabeth Elliot silently nodded, wondering if young people could ever truly understand the dimensions of what they demanded of the old.

13

Most people really believe that the Christian commandments (e.g., to love one's neighbor as oneself) are intentionally a little too severe—like putting the clock ahead half an hour to make sure of not being late in the morning.

Kierkegaard

They had, indeed, reached what Meghan had described as Richland's finest motel, called, perhaps not surprisingly, the Hanford House. Elizabeth had been more than grateful to immediately sit in the establishment's dining room, resting and looking through the sweeping plate-glass windows at the strong and broad Columbia flowing just yards away. Meghan, after ordering, had disappeared to register them. When she returned, she reported they had a room with a view of the river, and that she had already seen it and settled Panda down there.

"There were some standard-issue crackers and peanuts in the room," said Meghan. "I took the liberty of giving your allotment as well as mine to Panda. And I'll bring him something from this to round it off," she added just as their brunch orders arrived.

"How did you manage to register us under false names," asked Elizabeth quietly after the waitress had departed, "when your credit card has your real name?"

"I sure didn't show them my plastic!" responded Meghan

as she shoveled food into her mouth. "I just gave 'em greenbacks."

"In New England, I think any inn would ask for credit cards as well as other identification," said Elizabeth. "But this is, surely, quite a different place." She methodically but gladly cleaned her plate. With a pot of hot tea to comfort her, and energy from the food rushing into her bloodstream, she felt much better, but also deeply tired. She took a double dose of arthritis medicine as Meghan finished her coffee.

"I need to rest," Elizabeth said simply.

"Fine," answered Meghan. "I'm pretty hazy myself, despite this java. And my arm is acting up. Let's go to our room and sack out, while housekeeping washes these clothes we have on."

To the financially cautious Elizabeth, the idea of hiring someone to do her laundry seemed extravagant, but she was far too tired to protest. Besides, they needed both rest and clean clothes. Buying both at the same time might be expensive, but in and of itself it could not be wrong.

Elizabeth slowly and stiffly stood. Meghan helped her with her good arm, and they walked to their room. The younger woman spoke briefly to Panda as she gave him what food she had brought. Then she announced an intention to shower, and Panda curled up by the door to the hallway.

Elizabeth undressed, laying her filthy clothes at the foot of one of the two double beds in the spacious room. She crawled between the clean sheets of her bed, reflecting ruefully that she was, in a sense, homeless, and for the moment without possessions. Poverty, she knew, was one of the classic paths to spiritual life. Although she was not, of course, actually poor, her situation made it clear that she must depend on Meghan's strength and wits, and on the will of God. Elizabeth was no stranger to the process of seeking God's will, and she was capable of calmly putting herself at risk for its sake. But just as she was considering how she should pray, an all too familiar black-and-white spot danced into her field of view.

Oh no! she thought. *Not now.*

The sparkling area in her vision grew larger, and she knew she was headed for a migraine headache. Getting out of bed, she took some of the painkillers the pharmacy had given her.

"I'll be asleep for a while, Panda," she said to the dog, who looked at her alertly. "I'm really not well just now. Don't let anything happen without me, will you?"

Panda studied Elizabeth as she returned to bed. The last sound Elizabeth heard was the running and splashing water of Meghan's shower.

A long time later, Elizabeth blinked, opened her eyes, and took an inventory of herself. The pain in her head, so intense at some points during her troubled sleep, was wholly gone. She did not know where she was, but she knew that a lot of time had passed since she had gone to bed. Her mind was groggy, owing to the narcotic, but she slowly put on her glasses and sat up.

A wide, strongly flowing river cut across the view from the window. It was beautiful, but the sunlight dancing on its surface bothered Elizabeth's eyes. She looked away from the bright lights and studied the pleasant but sterile room. Only as Panda stepped over to greet her did she remember the fire at Meghan's trailer, their retreat to Richland, and her collapse in this bed.

"I'm glad to see thee," she said sincerely to the dog, reaching out to scratch his head. "You are one of the few constants in my life lately."

The shaggy dog gave one thump of his tail on the carpet.

Getting out of bed, Elizabeth discovered her clothes, clean and fresh, stacked on a chair. A note from Meghan lay on top of them:

> Elizabeth:
>
> You're still out cold, which I guess means you need the rest. I've had a nap, and feel much better. I'm going to get a rental car at the place across the street. I want to go back to the trailer court and see if there's anything at all to be salvaged. The embers will be cool by now.
>
> I'll talk to my neighbors. Someone may well have seen something; it's a tight-knit trailer court—the way working-class housing often is. There are a lot of kids and long-term residents, and a stranger stopping by in the early morning would be noticed. So I'm hopeful.
>
> I'm not sure why, but Panda really wants to stay here. So I'll leave him to watch over you. I think he's adopting you as one of his sheep.
>
> I'll see you both by six or seven tonight. You'll be right here, OK?
>
> Meghan

P.S. Don't let anybody into the room while I'm gone. Just ignore any knocks or phone calls. Panda will be fine until I come back.

A glance at her watch showed Elizabeth it was already after five o'clock. She drew a hot bath for herself, soaked in it for a few minutes, and washed her hair using the shampoo provided by the Hanford House. She dressed without much pain, and was truly relieved to be clean once again.

Turning on the television, she changed channels at random until she struck upon the local evening news. There was no mention of an intrusion during the night at the Hanford site, no acknowledgment that shots had been fired. There was, however, a report about a meeting between state environmental officials and Hanford representatives. The issues under discussion seemed to involve the details of a response to a federal government report released earlier, and Elizabeth could not really follow what was said.

But the anchorwoman on the program did briefly mention a trailer-court fire west of Richland, a blaze to which the county's volunteer force had responded. The cause of the fire, the anchorwoman said, was under investigation. A string of local advertisements were followed by the weather report. Elizabeth turned off the television. Just then, there was a knock on the door, and a voice called Elizabeth's name.

"It's me," said the person outside the door. "Open up, Elizabeth. I've a lot to tell you."

The old Quaker rose carefully to her feet and took a few steps toward the door. She stopped, however, when she saw that Panda was standing alert beside the doorframe, making no sign he recognized the voice. Quickly thinking back, Elizabeth wasn't sure that what she had heard had been a woman's voice, although it had been pitched high. She stood quietly. Looking over her glasses, she saw that there was no peephole in the door. The thick carpet in the room, she knew, made it unlikely she could see anything under the door, even if she could get down on her knees without making noise.

Elizabeth sat on the edge of the bed near the door and whispered, "Quiet!" to Panda.

The knocking was repeated, more loudly, but this time no one called into the room. After a moment, Elizabeth thought she heard steps moving down the hall. She remained sitting on the bed, without making a sound, and let minutes pass in receptive waiting. The sheepdog followed her example.

A while later, there was a quick rap on the door. A voice called out, "It's me, Elizabeth. Are you awake?"

Panda stood up and industriously wagged his tail, so Elizabeth opened the door. It was Meghan, who quickly stepped inside, said hello to Elizabeth, and knelt down to her dog.

"Big news!" she said happily. "When I got back home, the neighbors had a lot to say. A couple of the kids had seen someone stop by the court this morning. Apparently he parked on the highway and walked in. The kids were curious, and got a good look at him and the car. The neighbors said Tomlinson had taken the kids into Prosser, and I hightailed it out there. I was afraid our fine sheriff and his deputies might find some way of hushing the witnesses. But when I got there, the sheriff told me he'd used the kids' description, and your earlier one, to get a warrant for our friend Al Cartwright. He was put in a lineup while I was there." She smiled broadly. "Both kids, independently, picked him out, no sweat. So he's in a cell in the courthouse right now, charged with arson."

"I'm glad," said Elizabeth simply. "That's one part of the picture that's resolved."

"But I don't know how we can show he shot Rebe," continued Meghan, shaking her head. "Arson is a serious charge, and it will keep him out of circulation for now, but nothing approaching justice is possible until we can show what happened to Rebecca—and who ordered it."

Elizabeth related the story of the knock on the door a few minutes earlier.

"The person who knocked called you Elizabeth, you're sure?" queried the young doctor, using her briskest doctor-to-patient voice.

"Yes," said Elizabeth, "I'm sure. But I'm not sure if it was a man's or a woman's voice. Panda knew it wasn't you, but that's all that was clear."

"Jesus!" Meghan slumped down into a chair. "They followed us here, I guess, when we walked down George Washington Way. I can't see how else they could identify us, with my truck parked up at the pharmacy and me checking us in under different names. But I didn't see anyone on the street, did you?"

"I didn't notice anyone following us," answered Elizabeth, "but I'm sure I'm not alert to such things."

"I'll be damned," said Meghan, idly scratching Panda's head. "The Hanford boys are more organized, and more surreptitious, than I would have believed. I was careful when I came back here. I parked over beyond the fire station, on a side street, then walked in a kind of crazy pattern. The small streets, at least, were empty. But I guess that's all for nothing."

"What would have happened if I had opened the door?" mused Elizabeth.

"We don't want to know," said Meghan flatly. She stood up, glancing around the room. "We've got to get out of here, that's for sure. Let's go out the door toward the river. If our escorts are in the lobby or the parking lot, they probably saw me arrive. We don't have time to spare."

"Happily," Elizabeth observed dryly, "we don't have a lot to take with us."

The two women went down the stairs to the first floor and out the back door of the building, toward the river. Panda stayed one step behind Meghan, literally following at her heels. They saw no one, and they quickly walked away from the Hanford House. A paved path ran along the riverbank, and they turned in the upriver direction. A steady trickle of people passed them, women with babies in strollers, a pair of Rollerblading teenagers, a ten-year-old on a bicycle. The banks of the Columbia, it was clear, served as a linear park and a place to promenade before the setting of the sun. Meghan looked behind them every minute or so, but said she could see no one other than people who looked as if they belonged on the paved path.

Elizabeth was glad to discover that the long, deep nap and her medications had made her more limber. She walked slowly but, by her standards, easily. Even her knees were not too painful. Still, she knew she could not keep going long.

"What sense does it make to surreptitiously follow us to that inn and try to enter our room, but then not follow us now?" she asked.

"I dunno." Meghan frowned and looked at Elizabeth. "I was just wondering if we're succumbing to paranoia. It would be easy enough, around here. But there are so many objective things, a long list of them besides murder: Rebe's car being trashed, my trailer burning down, and someone knowing your name and room number at a motel where we were staying under pseudonyms."

A quaint wooden bench, painted dark green, was coming up on their left. Elizabeth set her sights on it.

"I don't understand it all, but I do know we can't literally outrun them," she said. "This looks like a place to rest and think for a moment. There are enough people around that it must be safe."

"OK," said Meghan, "you sit here. I'll circle back and get the rental car. We need wheels."

Elizabeth had gratefully, if stiffly, sat on the bench. Panda immediately sat beside her, apparently studying the seagulls circling over the river.

"Seagulls in a desert," mused Elizabeth. "And plutonium produced next to this gorgeous river. Richland is full of contradictions."

"Panda, stay!" said Meghan. The young woman turned away and left at a trot, calling, "I'll be right back, Elizabeth."

"She'll come back for us," said Elizabeth warmly to Panda. But there was no need to worry about the dog. He had heard his mistress say he should stay, and he was intent on doing so. Elizabeth idly patted his head, and her hand slipped down his long neck. Suddenly, Panda jerked his head away from her.

"How could I have hurt you?" said Elizabeth in wonder. "You must have a tick bite, Panda. Are there ticks in this desert?"

Gently she explored the fur in the area that had produced such a strong response. There seemed to be nothing unusual, and the dog was quiet. But Elizabeth felt a prick on one of her fingers. She quickly drew her hand away.

"Have you got something sharp buried in your fur?" she asked the dog in puzzlement.

Panda submitted to further investigation. Elizabeth's stiff but gentle fingers soon rediscovered the small, sharp object in the long fur. Something was under Panda's leather collar.

"Raise your head for me, would you, my friend?" said Elizabeth. The dog allowed his head to be raised by the slight pressure of her hand. She unbuckled his collar.

Although the sun was now nearly setting, the light was more than sufficiently strong to see a narrow, apparently electronic device taped under the weather-beaten collar. A short metal protrusion at one end had been the source of the pricks to both dog and human.

Elizabeth sighed. She remembered the thin man in dark clothes who had run his hands over Panda's head and neck in the pharmacy parking lot. The dog, as she recalled, had suddenly growled.

"It's all a little more clear," she said to Panda, trying to encourage herself.

She stood up and looked around. A few steps away from the river, a city street ended in a cul-de-sac. A garbage truck was rumbling down the street toward the river. Elizabeth told Panda to stay where he was, then walked over to a garbage can standing near the curb. Peeling the tracking device off the collar, she contributed it to the trash.

"That's a fine place for such an item," she said to herself.

Returning to the dog and the riverside path, she sat down again on the bench and rebuckled Panda's collar around his neck. Scratching the dog behind the ears, she watched as the garbagemen progressed down the short street. In a minute, the electronic device had been transferred to the back of the truck. The men scrambled up to their posts on the bumper, and the heavy vehicle rumbled away.

"At least we're done with that," murmured Elizabeth softly to the dog.

Just then, a honking car made her turn. Inside a dark gray sedan, Meghan was waving. Elizabeth called to Panda, and the two of them went to the car. After hearing Meghan's voice, Panda was more than willing to jump into the back-seat.

"Did you see anyone while I was gone?" asked Meghan after Elizabeth had taken a seat in the small car.

"Several people, but all of the sort you'd expect here. But I found something that surprised me." Elizabeth explained about her discovery in Panda's collar, and her disposal of the device in the city's garbage truck.

"I'll be damned," Meghan retorted as she turned the car around and accelerated toward the main street. "I guess we weren't paranoid. You hear stories of how incompetent the feds are, but the security boys at Hanford are pretty well organized, at that." She continued without giving the Quaker a chance to respond. "If this car is still clean, and I'm hopeful it is, the men of the Rat Patrol will follow the garbage truck. If they get all the way to the dump, of course, they'll realize what's happened. By then, we'd better be far away from here."

14

Only our concept of time makes it possible for us to speak of the Day of Judgment by that name; in reality it is a summary court in perpetual session.

Franz Kafka

"Where can we go?" asked Elizabeth. For the first time, it occurred to her that she might simply leave Washington State. Cambridge, after all, was her home, the place where her life, and her true responsibilities, lay. She wasn't suited to the tactics of espionage, and the world within Hanford, it was now fully clear, was almost beyond her comprehension.

Involuntarily she murmured, "I need to pray."

"What?" asked Meghan distractedly, but she didn't pause for an answer. "We should go to Rebe's house. There's really no place else. My home is gone, and we can't expose Nancy's kids to danger from the goons who've been following us here in Richland."

As Meghan spoke she made a couple of sharp turns, studying the rearview mirror. Elizabeth, who was beginning to form her own ideas about Rebecca's murder, only observed in reply, "The Nicholses' farmhouse may be quite dangerous."

"I suppose so. I mean, I can see that if the enforcers working for the feds tried to get at you in a motel in busy Richland, an isolated farmhouse outside little ol' Benton City could be a lot worse."

Meghan accelerated onto the broad lanes of the interstate. "But I'm no pacifist, and I plan to survive the night," she said grimly. "So will you if you stick with me. I'll drive all the way to Prosser, to make sure we've ditched the Hanford goons, then stop somewhere and buy a rifle."

"Surely one can't just buy such an item, like picking up a jug of milk!" exclaimed Elizabeth wonderingly.

"Why not? There's no waiting period for rifles, like there is for handguns. And it's hunting season, anyway, so what could be more normal?"

The Quaker sighed quietly. She saw the car in which she sat as hurtling toward some evil purpose. She knew, of course, that times of intense passion did not represent good opportunities to witness to the power of nonviolence. She wondered how she could express her bedrock moral and religious values without immediately alienating her young friend.

"A doctor," she observed finally, "might find—when the time came—that it was impossible to use a gun against a person. At least, I would guess that could be the case. A life devoted to healing, like yours is, Meghan, is a higher calling, something that can shape every action throughout life."

"I'm a child of the rural Northwest, Elizabeth," responded Meghan quickly. "I'll always be a northwesterner first, only then a doctor." She switched on the headlights. "But, I'll grant you, we should call the sheriff as soon as we can. You two seem to be on the same wavelength, so I'll let you do the talking. You can tell him we were followed, tell him about the knock on the door of the motel, and about Panda's collar."

Elizabeth nodded. "I can ask that we be put in protective custody."

To the Quaker, being locked up looked like a good way to defuse the violence gathering around them. Even though such a fix could only be temporary, protective custody would give everyone a chance to think. And Elizabeth would have time to pray.

But the world has always been infused with different realities for different people.

"No!" barked Meghan to Elizabeth's suggestion. All of her youthful, indignant anger had returned. "No protective custody! We've got to stay out here, and stay active. It's the only way we'll trap them into making more mistakes, like they made with my trailer. If we quit now, Elizabeth, Rebe's death will go unavenged."

"Vengeance is not ours," answered Elizabeth, paraphrasing the words of the Bible in a form that she hoped an unchurched young person might understand.

But her message was instantly deflected.

"Maybe 'vengeance' is not the word," said Meghan. "But we both want to bring Rebe's killers to justice. Those men have got to answer for what they did—and what they're still doing right now in Richland. It's not just one incident, Elizabeth. These guys have been brazen criminals for decades. They subvert our constitutional rights, and mislead the public over and over. If they never have to answer for all of that, it's no wonder that the kooks among them end up as outright thugs and killers. And that feeds into pretty extreme responses against the government. Places like Hanford have really made the militia movement bloom, if you ask me!"

Meghan wound down as she checked the car's rearview mirror. "This is my home. Right here in the inland Northwest. Killers of any kind have got to answer for what they've done. And I don't mean answering for it on some distant day of judgment in some other world. No offense."

"None taken," responded Elizabeth, dryly but truthfully. "And I do agree that we must answer for all we do. Including answering for what we do in the pursuit of justice."

The two women watched the last sliver of the burnt-orange sun slip behind the distant mountains that lay directly in front of them. Behind them, in the small rear seat of the car, Panda whined briefly.

"It's OK, pup," said Meghan. "We're well away from Richland, and the 'coyotes' aren't following us."

Panda audibly sighed, then lay down again with a soft grunt.

The two women lapsed into silence. It seemed the best way to preserve the peace, at least for the present.

As the rented car raced through the night, Elizabeth realized her eyelids were drooping.

This is no time for fatigue! she chided herself.

Elizabeth sat up as straight as she could, then took several deep breaths. But the afteraffects of a major dose of narcotics, on the one hand, and the grogginess that can follow in the wake of adrenaline, on the other, were not to be denied.

The combined soporific forces easily overwhelmed the old Quaker. Within minutes, she slid into a confused but quite deep sleep.

Elizabeth awoke with a start. The world around her was silent. She struggled for a moment to understand what part of Cambridge could look like this poorly lit gravel parking lot. Turning to see behind her, she recognized the shape of the white patch of fur on Panda's face. Instantly, she remembered everything she needed to know.

"What an old cripple I am," she said to Panda, reaching out to ruffle his fur. "Good for nothing except sleep."

From the midst of the darkness Elizabeth heard the comforting sound of the dog's tail beating time against the backseat.

"I think I've become glad to see thee," murmured Elizabeth, "simply because the reverse is always the case. Unmerited adoration, Panda, is quite agreeable."

The sound of the car trunk opening made Panda's head spin around. Elizabeth, out of arthritic necessity, turned forward in her seat as the trunk closed. In an instant, Meghan opened the driver's door and threw herself behind the wheel. As she did so she thrust a small item onto Elizabeth's lap.

"Glad to see you two!" Meghan said as she started the small car's engine. "It was getting lonely on the highway with both of you asleep."

Elizabeth nodded her acceptance of what she took as a peace offering meant to blunt the emotional edge of their earlier disagreement.

"Where are we?" she asked in an even tone.

"Outside of Prosser," replied Meghan, steering the car off the gravel of the parking lot and onto rough blacktop. She accelerated as she added, "I know the owner of that little place. Joe McGreevy. I doctored one of his kids last year—both legs smashed up in a car wreck, but walking OK now."

"Should I assume there is a weapon in the trunk?" asked Elizabeth steadily.

"Just a hunting rifle—the semiautomatic kind," came the reply. The Quaker was silently trying to digest this information when Meghan added, "Don't worry, Elizabeth. It's only for defending ourselves. I wouldn't use it any other way."

"We all like to *think* of such actions in those terms," agreed Elizabeth, "even on the national level. That's why the 'War Department' became the 'Department of Defense.' " She added with an uncharacteristic note of urgency, "I hope I'm not holding ammunition on my lap!"

"No," replied Meghan quickly. "I wouldn't ask you to do that. I can respect Quakers, you see, even though I think your approach to a lot of things is sort of crazy."

"Thank you," said Elizabeth with a hint of dry sarcasm.

The younger woman, however, busy rejoining the interstate, hardly heard the Quaker's soft reply.

"What you've got there," Meghan continued when she had completed the traffic maneuver, "is a cell phone that I borrowed from Mr. McGreevy. I was hoping you'd call the sheriff."

"Good," said Elizabeth warmly. "That's an excellent idea. But how do I use this?"

With instructions from Meghan, Elizabeth mastered the

basics of cell-phone mechanics and, eventually, reached the information operator. Repeating the sheriff's number aloud, over and over, she redialed. In just a moment, the office put her through to Mr. Tomlinson himself.

With a few pauses to organize her scattered thoughts, Elizabeth calmly explained all that had happened to her and to Panda in the city of Richland. The old Quaker felt a bit disoriented rushing down the interstate while talking on the telephone. But the connection was clear enough, and the longer she spoke, the more natural it felt.

"Where is Dr. Zillann's truck now?" asked the sheriff when Elizabeth had finished relating her tale.

Elizabeth explained.

"I'll send a man over," said Tomlinson. "The dog's collar is probably gone, but the truck will be waiting in the pharmacy's parking lot. My boy can check for transmitters. That would be a nice piece of hard evidence, although it wouldn't conclusively link—"

The sheriff's voice dissolved into a soft hum.

"I'm sorry," said Elizabeth quickly. "I missed the last part of what you said."

But even the humming of the cell phone faded into silence.

"Let me have it," said Meghan. After a moment of one-handed examination, she tossed it down to the gap in the bucket seats between them. "The battery is dead. Happens quite a lot with these cheap jobs, I'm afraid."

"Oh!" ejaculated Elizabeth in dismay. "We do so need the sheriff's help!"

"I'm not going into protective custody," Meghan said instantly. "Don't even think it. But I'm glad that he's going to check my truck."

"So you trust a government official enough to value his search of your pickup?" asked Elizabeth, perhaps with a hint of amusement in her voice.

"Tomlinson got Cartwright off the road," answered Meghan seriously. "That got my attention."

The car skimmed along through the darkness of the interstate. Elizabeth, who because of naps and narcotics had lost track of time, tried to look at her watch. There wasn't enough light, however, for her to see its face.

"Getting hungry?" asked Meghan.

"I think so." Elizabeth tried to gauge what her body actually needed. It had been, she realized, a long time since they had had brunch at the Hanford House on the Columbia. "This has surely been a topsy-turvy day," she sighed.

"If we keep up this schedule," agreed the younger woman with a nod, "we'll trim down a good bit!"

"You don't need to," Elizabeth countered automatically but truthfully.

"To tell the truth, I picked up a little junk food at Joe's," said Meghan. "Don't inform the AMA, would you? I thought a few 'empty calories' could keep us going, since there's no place to stop out here for a proper meal. But I'm afraid the food is in the trunk, in the sack with the ammo."

Elizabeth immediately lost her appetite.

Meghan took the Benton City exit, and the smooth pavement of the interstate fell away behind them. The uneven blacktop of a state highway led them through the tiny hamlet, then passed Lincoln and Pamela's trailer and out into the deep darkness of a rural Northwest night. In a couple of minutes, Meghan turned the car into the long gravel drive that led to the Nicholses' old family house. She guided the small car up the driveway and then, moving very slowly, steered it around the back of the house out of sight from the road.

"Goodness!" said Elizabeth. "I hadn't thought about it, but how are we going to get in the house?"

"First things first," responded the young doctor, dousing the car's headlights and turning off the engine. "You stay here, Elizabeth." Her voice shifted tones as she added, "Panda, come!"

The collie scrambled out of the car through Meghan's open door, which Meghan then swung shut. As Elizabeth's eyes adjusted to the darkness she heard the trunk being opened. Several minutes ticked by, during which she had both time to surmise that Meghan was loading her rifle and time to ask herself how a Quaker could have ended up a housebreaker in the company of an armed young person.

One short bark from Panda roused Elizabeth's attention. She opened her car door and was instantly rewarded by rays from the car's dome light. Getting stiffly out of the car, she stood awkwardly on the gravel.

"Shhh!" said Meghan from the corner of the house.

Elizabeth softly pulled the car door back to a nearly closed position. The dome light clicked off, and she left the door resting against its latch. Cautiously, she moved toward her companion.

"Judging from the engine noise," said Meghan softly as

Elizabeth joined her, "a pretty big vehicle just pulled into the drive out front."

Elizabeth's heart skipped a beat.

"I should tell you what I've been thinking about Rebe's murder," she began quietly.

"Shhh!" responded Meghan, perhaps a little harshly. Her thin young body strained as she leaned forward around the corner of the house.

Accepting the command for silence, the Quaker looked around for a glimpse of Panda. She thought she saw a familiar patch of white fur ahead of them, but as she blinked it disappeared into the darkness of the desert. Meghan's much nearer shape, Elizabeth saw as she silently studied it, included a heavy slash of an even deeper darkness by her side. It was, Elizabeth assumed, the rifle—now loaded to kill. Automatically she noted it was the ungainly, thicker kind of rifle. She sighed involuntarily.

"He had his lights out before he pulled in," said Meghan softly, "and he cut his engine as soon as he could. Now, judging by what Panda's doing, he's out somewhere in front of the house."

Elizabeth, despite feeling miserably cold, idly wondered why the unknown person should be assigned the masculine pronoun. Men, she often thought, were unfairly given too many evil roles in the minds of women. But her thoughts were cut short by the physical impulse to move; she was growing too cold to remain where she was.

Quietly Elizabeth turned around and walked along the length of the back of Rebecca's childhood home. With the help of a little moonlight, she cautiously picked her way past their parked car and to the far back corner of the house. Stopping, she peered forward into the night. She could see little, and heard only the sound of the night breeze blowing across the sparse vegetation. Feeling better, both because she was moving and because she was away from Meghan's gun, the Quaker walked slowly and softly toward the front corner of the house. Reaching it without incident, she looked across the front portion of the property.

The long gravel drive on the far side of the house and the desert beyond were immersed in the deepness of the night. But just in front of the house stood the large, square shape of an American-made pickup truck. At the sight of it, Elizabeth involuntarily nodded to herself. She was, quite suddenly, back on familiar ground, almost as clearly as if she had been instantly transported back to Cambridge.

Just then, from beyond the pickup, Elizabeth saw the beam of a flashlight. It played back and forth across the ground, apparently guided by the hand of someone intent on searching this patch of the desert floor.

With a calm inspired by the certainty of understanding, Elizabeth stepped forward. "Good evening," she said steadily.

The flashlight turned toward her, and in an instant Elizabeth was all but blinded by the beam on her face.

"You!" said Lincoln's voice, taut with fear. "What are you doing here!"

"I could ask you the same question," said Elizabeth calmly, "but I think I know the answer. You left something here when you shot your cousin, didn't you?"

"So you found it!" sputtered Lincoln, suddenly more angry than afraid. Then, belatedly and with apparent confusion, "I don't know what you're talking about, Mrs. Elliot."

"You most certainly do," responded Elizabeth quietly. "The only question in my mind is why you committed such a horrible act. I'm sure you're not an evil nor a cold-blooded man. And I imagine you've been tormented, day and night, the past couple of days." She tried to take a step toward Lincoln, but the light in her eyes made it too likely she would stumble, perhaps badly, so she stayed where she was. "But Reb had become a threat to you, Lincoln, hadn't she? That's what led to this terrible event. Rebecca was a danger to everything in your future."

"Not just mine," answered Lincoln slowly. The beam of the flashlight slid slowly from Elizabeth's face to the ground in front of her. He sighed in the darkness. "If it was just me, maybe it would have been different. But I've got a wife to provide for. And I don't want her and me becoming a burden to my son."

"Your property is all you have, isn't it?" Elizabeth nodded. "No pension, no bank accounts. Just Social Security and your parcel of land."

"If Reba had had any sense—or any family loyalty—she wouldn't have insisted on mucking around with those samples. I told her when I got here that I needed to get the wife and me to an easier climate for retirement. It's all that we've hoped and planned for over the years."

"Rebecca's research, I suppose," mused Elizabeth quietly, "might have pushed all the land values around here to zero."

She shifted her weight from one foot to the other but nevertheless began to shiver.

"You bet," agreed Lincoln. "And you're right about the torment, too. I've been sick at heart since that evening. But Reba was so stubborn! She just didn't care what her crazy Seattle ideas could do to her own flesh and blood right here." He heaved a sigh. "It was a semiauto I had in the truck, you see. So the shell must have ejected. That's been haunting me, but I had to wait to search for it until the deputy's watch over this place finally ended."

"Hold it right there, both of you!" screamed a voice from somewhere in the darkness. "Don't move or you're dead!"

Panda's white patch of fur appeared near the pool of light in front of Elizabeth. He stepped toward her, tail swishing in recognition.

"I hope I'm ready for death," Elizabeth said steadily to the night, "but I doubt you mean to shoot me, Meghan."

"Elizabeth?" asked Meghan incredulously.

In just a moment, the night exploded in action. The pool of light in front of Elizabeth moved crazily, then disappeared. It was replaced by a short beam of light on the ground where, apparently, Lincoln had dropped the flashlight. Simultaneously, Panda spun around with a snarl. Meghan yelled, then grunted, as she and Lincoln struggled for her rifle. Finally, from down the highway in the direction of Benton City, two vehicles with red and blue lights raced into sight. In a flash, Elizabeth realized that the cars might belong to the sheriff's office—or they might be part of Hanford's security department.

15

Somehow we must learn not only to meet sorrow with courage, which is comparatively easy, but with serenity, which is more difficult, being not a single act but a way of living.

Daisy Newman
Twentieth-Century American Friend

Elizabeth had only an instant to act, but she took it, instinctively calling on God for help. As she did so, her ears were filled with a ferocious snarl from Panda. The collie sprang in front of Elizabeth and leaped high into the air toward his mistress and Lincoln, still locked in their struggle for the gun. Both humans fell, with the dog on top of them, and a deafening report ripped through the fabric of the desert night.

Elizabeth heard Panda, literally screaming in pain, as soon as her senses had recovered from the roar of the rifle. The dog, wailing piteously, dragged himself across the ground toward her. The injured animal, she saw, had only the use of its front shoulders and legs. His hindquarters dragged limply behind him in the dust. Elizabeth knelt beside the collie, automatically, if nonsensically, saying in her most soothing voice, "Good puppy, good puppy, good puppy!"

The official vehicles on the highway turned on their sirens, presumably in response to the rifle report. The cars turned into the gravel drive, and the siren wails, out of phase with each other and drawing quickly nearer, made it impossible for Elizabeth to hear her own voice. She knelt down still further over Panda, sitting fully on the cold ground, trying to offer him some protection from the assault of sound.

Powerful beams of light cutting across the sagebrush instantly appeared in Elizabeth's ground-level view. She was quickly blinded by one of them, a merciless light that isolated both her and the dog over which she was crouching protectively. In just a moment, Meghan materialized out of the darkness and almost pushed Elizabeth aside.

Only hours later, as Elizabeth reconstructed events in her memory, could she understand all that had happened next. The sirens were cut off, and a loudspeaker from one of the cars issued commands for everyone to hold still. The phrase "Drop that gun" was part of one command.

Another report from Meghan's rifle, now somewhere near the far corner of the house, cut through the night. It was answered by a long explosion of gunfire from the direction of the drive. During this hellish assault, Meghan threw herself on Elizabeth, forcing the older woman down to the ground next to Panda. Meghan's light body was on top of the Quaker and the collie both as the barrage died away and the loudspeaker once again called for everyone to freeze.

"I better not move," said Meghan to Elizabeth. "Are you OK under there?"

"Uh," grunted Elizabeth. It was all she could articulate at the time, but it communicated enough.

"Panda," called Meghan softly, but the collie beside Elizabeth was still and silent.

"Stay down!" shouted a familiar voice from the nearer

darkness. Elizabeth, with Meghan still partially on top of her, had no choice but to obey. Then, in a different pitch, the man's voice called, "Jess, you go up to him really slow. We'll cover you from here."

In a moment a young voice sang out, "It's OK, I've got his rifle. I think he's dead."

"Panda!" called Meghan again, softly but urgently.

Elizabeth felt the weight on top of her diminish, and she breathed more freely. Meghan was now kneeling next to her, at the collie's shaggy head. Slowly, stiffly, Elizabeth struggled to sit up. With a determined heave and the help of a large and strong pair of hands, she found herself sitting on the desert dirt. Only then did she become aware that her side was covered with a warm, sticky liquid.

"Are you two OK?" asked Sheriff Tomlinson beside her.

"Yes," answered Elizabeth. "And we are glad to see thee."

But Meghan's sobs arrested any further words from Elizabeth.

"Panda, Panda! I'm sorry, Panda!" wailed the young woman, raising her head and addressing the darkness above them.

"Are you hit, Mrs. Elliot?" asked the sheriff, seeing for the first time her bloody side.

"No," said Elizabeth. "It's the collie. He was shot when Meghan's rifle went off, just as you came into view on the main road. Meghan and Lincoln were struggling for the gun, you see, and Panda leaped into the fray."

Tomlinson was looking toward his deputy near the house.

"The man you've shot," explained Elizabeth, "is Lincoln Wilkinson, my friend Rebecca's cousin and also her killer.

He had come back here to look for—what is it called? The thick-style rifles drop part of their bullet when they are fired, yes?"

"The shell casing," replied Tomlinson slowly, puzzled by the adjective Elizabeth had employed to describe a type of rifle. "But Lincoln's truck has a single-shot rifle in it. It's still there, in his cab—I saw it as we pulled up behind his vehicle. A rifle like that doesn't discharge any shells."

"I'll take your word for it," responded Elizabeth. "But when Rebecca introduced me to Lincoln, his truck had the thicker kind of rifle hanging across the rear window of the cab. You know, with a big piece hanging down from the middle. It has been gone from there in the days since Rebe's death, replaced by the thinner kind, just one long rodlike shape. The thick versus thin style is all I can distinguish when I see guns in the racks across the back of pickup cabs. And even that is more than I want to think about when it comes to guns. Anyway, the change in Lincoln's rifle was one clue for me, you see."

Elizabeth next briefly sketched the circumstances and motive for Rebecca's killing, relaying the main points of Lincoln's confession to the sheriff. Meghan, although still crying, grew quieter. The younger woman stroked Panda's head, which she held in her lap.

"Rebecca's death," continued Elizabeth, "was muddled, over and over again, by the actions of the men at Hanford. They dropped her off at her home on the day of her death, I'm sure. For reasons that only a defensive bureaucracy can fathom, they later denied any knowledge she had been on their property. I think that just may have been some reflex on their part, but I'm not sure. But anyway, after dropping her off, they worried they hadn't intimidated her sufficiently to make her stop her activities. So the next day, quite unaware of her death, they vandalized her car and stole the soil samples she had collected."

"And then linked her to you and Dr. Zillann, and torched the doctor's trailer," said Tomlinson with a nod. "At least we've got them on that one."

"Well," responded Elizabeth quietly, "you've got one of the smallest of the fishes, perhaps. Others of his ilk followed us around Richland later that day. Only the Lord knows what might have happened if they had got into our room when I was alone at the motel." Glancing at Meghan, she added, "But that's enough talk for now, isn't it, Mr. Tomlinson?"

The sheriff nodded.

Meghan was still steadily weeping next to Elizabeth. The older woman reached out and put her arms around the younger woman's shoulders.

"I know it's difficult," murmured Elizabeth. "He was so faithful."

"Boss!" called a young deputy, running toward them from the house. "The guy we hit has still got a pulse. Bill is calling over the radio for paramedics."

"It will be forever before they get out here," observed Tomlinson to the darkness.

Meghan, her arms around the collie's neck and head, continued to sob quietly.

"Doctor!" said Elizabeth sharply. "You must get up! A man needs you."

"Leave me alone!" Meghan choked out.

"No!" said Elizabeth firmly. "I won't! We require a doctor. You are that doctor. You have no choice, Dr. Zillann. Your training is desperately needed."

Without verbal response, Meghan let go of Panda and jerked to her feet, still raggedly weeping. The sheriff leaned down and helped Elizabeth to stand. By the time the older woman was up, Meghan had already walked to the corner of the house where Lincoln lay. The young doctor knelt down to the gravely injured man, turning briefly to wipe her tear-stained face on her upper arm as she did so.

"I think he was hit twice," she said as the sheriff and Elizabeth came up to her. Meghan's voice was still distorted by grief, but a doctor's sense of command and responsibility was rapidly asserting itself in her small, shaken frame.

"One bullet to this thigh," she continued, "one in the neck. Tomlinson, squat down here and apply pressure to his leg."

The big man dropped obediently to his knees.

"Double up your hanky, and here, man, push steadily. Just use one hand on it."

The sheriff struggled to keep up with the doctor's orders as Elizabeth stood silently by.

"Now take your other hand," barked Meghan crisply, "and push here, inside his leg. Good. Don't let up on the pressure in either place. Got it?"

Tomlinson grunted assent.

"The neck wound is a lot worse," said Meghan flatly, "but I'll do what I can. Elizabeth, have one of the deputies call into town by radio. There's only one hospital in Richland. Ask them to check for any record they have on Lincoln

Wilkinson. He's lived here his entire life, so they probably have something. If they know his blood type, tell them to have several units on hand in the ER when we get there."

Elizabeth stepped toward the cars pulled up on the long driveway. As she walked she had time for a brief prayer of thanksgiving for Meghan's return to her vocation. And the old Quaker unabashedly added a prayer for Panda, too. The dog, she reflected, might well have saved Meghan's life—and perhaps her own as well.

In Elizabeth's view, Panda had lived fully in the present, and with the freedom that only a complete commitment can bring. Rationally or not, Elizabeth Elliot commended the collie's spirit to the heavens.

16

In our desperate search for our destination . . . we may have overlooked the supreme importance of the question: Whence come ye? It may well be that the end is in the beginning; the beginning in the end.

Elfrida Vipont Foulds
Twentieth-Century English Friend

Despite the fog and rain, the plane had taken off from Seattle on time. Sheriff Tomlinson, who had driven Elizabeth across the desert and over the Cascades, had seen her off at the airport.

"Think it over again in a few weeks," he had said at parting. "I took down Lincoln's confession in the hospital, so that matter is cleared up. I've got Cartwright nailed on the arson charge, which is good. But there's still no physical evidence I can use for any criminal case against Hanford's security department and the men in charge of it."

He had shifted his weight from one foot to the other as he and Elizabeth looked out through the plate-glass windows of the terminal. His leather gun belt had squeaked softly, but Elizabeth had become so acclimated to the sound she hardly noticed it.

"You have options, Mrs. Elliot," the sheriff had continued in a businesslike tone. "You can retain a lawyer and sue Hanford in civil court for violation of your constitutional rights.

They tracked you with an electronic device, invading your privacy again and again. You and Dr. Zillann could call witnesses from within Hanford, and they would have to testify under oath. No matter how the case came out, it would be a warning shot across their bow. A lot of us in the neighborhood would be glad for something like that."

Elizabeth had politely promised to consider legal recourse, but she had little love for the workings of the law, and she could not embrace the firing of a warning shot, even as a metaphor. Before the conversation had gone any further, her row number had been called, and Elizabeth had boarded the airplane to begin the first leg of her long flight eastward.

Now, with a tepid cup of tea in one hand and the Rocky Mountains falling away under the plane, Elizabeth continued the letter she was trying to write to Meghan. It was her first experience in writing a condolence note on the occasion of an animal's, rather than a person's, death. Her fingers, only mildly stiff with arthritis, curled around the pen for a few more lines.

> It is never easy to lose a friend, and Panda was a truly devoted companion. Although I'm not usually a dog lover, his spirit touched even me—so in some small way I may understand part of your loss. Do grieve, Meghan. One must.

Elizabeth leaned back in her seat, closed her eyes, and reflected that animals were spared the worst traps—cynicism and hopelessness—into which humans so often fell. Recalling all of her experiences in central Washington State, she felt a surge of envy for all furry creatures: their innocence could never be shattered.

But in a moment, shaking her head at her own thinking, the old Quaker rebuked herself for her faithlessness. *The sacred Spirit of God, alive so clearly in human beings, is worth the risks that living as a human entails*, she declared to herself. *But I admit, I've grown a bit out of touch with my real self on this trip. Without a community of believers around me, I'm not sure I could ever lead a Spirit-filled life.* With great longing, Elizabeth called up a mental image of the Quaker Meetinghouse in Cambridge. Its simple form, and the regular availability of silent, community worship within it, beckoned across the continent to the sojourning Quaker. Elizabeth sighed, relaxing with the idea that she would soon be home and would take up her role as a member of Friends Meeting at Cambridge. Her heart warmed with a steady gladness as she felt herself drawing closer to home.

Settling further in her seat, Elizabeth prayed for Lincoln. Then she focused her prayerful attention even more earnestly on all the people still working in various capacities in the government's installation at Hanford.